FOOL'S GOLD

April Harbringer

After the tragic death of her fiance
Celia knew she would never love again
and resigned herself to a life of hard
work and bittersweet memories. But
then Adam came—a man without a
past, whose memory was lost after an
accident at sea. Celia took him into
her home and her heart, he brought
joy into her life . . . a joy she thought
was lost forever. But who was Adam?
Celia feared that the past would reach
out and take him from her. Was
Adam's love the treasure Celia had
longed for . . . or was it just fool's
gold?

FOOL'S GOLD

April Harbringer

Curley Publishing, Inc.
Hampton, NH.

Library of Congress Cataloging-in-Publication Data

Harbringer, April.
  Fools's gold / by April Harbringer. – Large print ed.
  p. cm.
  "Curley large print."
  ISBN 0–7927–1333–8 (lg. print). – ISBN 0–7927–1332–X
  (softcover : lg. print)
  1. Large type books. I. Title
[PR6058.A619F6 1992]   92–16535
823'.914–dc20   CIP

Published by arrangement with Donald MacCampbell, Inc. in the United States, Canada, the U.K. and British Commonwealth and the rest of the world market.

Distributed in Great Britain, Ireland and the Commonwealth by Chivers Press Limited, Bath BA2 3AX, England.

Printed in Great Britain

FOOL'S GOLD

CHAPTER ONE

On the eve of the second anniversary of her fiance's death, Celia Walton tossed fitfully in her secluded farmhouse bedroom. The tail end of a wicked three-day storm was just beating itself out on the rugged coast outside and the whine of its wind grated agonizingly across the girl's nerves, bringing back the memories – and the tears.

She twisted once more in the darkness, then flipped on her yellow lamp. Somehow she had to keep the past at bay throughout the remainder of the darkness. In a few moments she was pacing the floor, running her fingers through her dark copper hair and trying not to hear again Gavin's merry shout that day he rowed away to try his luck at fishing in the sea. Only a headache had prevented her from going along. When she learned he had died, she had wished . . .

Yes, she had wished she had gone with him. She had wished she lay beside him at the bottom of the bay rather than remain behind to endure the misery his loss had inflicted upon her.

1

In the years that followed, Celia thought she had managed to deal with her grief. But the coming of the anniversary of Gavin's death had unearthed feelings she thought were long since buried.

By the first pale light of dawn, total exhaustion finally overcame the pain and made her collapse, all but asleep on her feet, into the enfolding comfort of the big four-poster bed.

When she did awaken, it was with the alarm, for brilliant sunshine streamed across the gay calico squares of her light quilt and a robin sang in the great maple outside. A glance at the clock made her gasp and leap for the worn jeans and green shirt draped neatly over the chair at her side. Breakfast would be long over. Uncle Bart would have the cows milked and the black and white calves would be sticking their heads through the rails for something to eat.

Barely smoothing her short, glossy curls, Celia dashed downstairs and was halfway across the worn kitchen linoleum before her Aunt Meg got her by the elbow.

"Slow down, girl, and have a cup of tea. It won't hurt Bart to feed the calves himself for once."

"But it's late. I ... slept in so."

"I know, I know." Sadness in the aging eyes made it clear Aunt Meg knew only too well how her niece had spent the night. "Just sit down.

2

I'll fix you some toast."

Celia gulped gratefully at the hot tea and immediately felt better. Brown toast with marmalade made her relax in this familiar old-fashioned kitchen she had first come to as a quivering, big-eyed girl of fourteen after the death of her parents. Her aunt and uncle, childless themselves, took her to their gruff, kindly hearts, regarding her from then on as their own.

But today there was no safety, even here. Buttering a second bit of toast, she looked at the sideboard – and thought once more of Gavin's handsome face.

Quickly, she looked away, not hungry any more. After a few bites for Aunt Meg's sake she pushed away the plate and stood up.

"I better get going. The cows should have been in the pasture long ago."

Outside, the scent of rainwashed grass and the clear joy of the sunlit hillsides seemed to mock her. It wasn't fair. She had known Gavin only five months, a mere five months before a cruel death had snatched him away from her for all time. Aunt Meg and Uncle Bart had sacrificed so that she might go to Toronto to study and to see a bit of the world. She had been completing her year honing her secretarial skills at the business college when she had met the young science teacher at a Christmas dance.

3

It had been a love built on rainbows and laughter. What fun they had going to shows and fascinating new restaurants. They had snowball fights and floundered gaily through snowdrifts in the park and into each other's arms. When spring came, Celia brought Gavin back to Nova Scotia for the wedding. The little church in the hollow had been reserved, the dress of ivory satin laid in readiness, the old parlor waxed and aired for the at-home reception.

Then one of the leathery fishermen of the coast had found the borrowed skiff upside down and half submerged. No one even expected to find a trace of Gavin's body.

"It's the currents," they said. "They take everything out to sea. A man would have to be a hero of a swimmer to make it to the shore."

Crushed and stunned, Celia had crept into the only shelter she knew, the security of the two old people who did their best, for the exciting jobs, the glittering life that had called before, vanished. Celia's one desire had been to numb herself with work on the farm, where an extra helping hand was so badly needed.

Determinedly, Celia wrenched her mind back to the present as she approached the milk cows crowding expectantly against the gate.

"Come on, girls," she smiled, "time the lot of you were on your way."

The pasture was a high field, sloping rapidly to the sea and shaded, here and there, by outposts of the dense hardwood forests native to the province. As was her habit after the cows were turned out, Celia slipped through the fence and took a shortcut back to the house via the narrow, sand-strewn strip of beach.

She walked, as she always did down there, with a certain air of defiance, eyeing the sea as one eyes a once trusted friend who has become an enemy. Yet she hadn't been walking two minutes before she knew that today, of all days, she shouldn't have taken this path. How could she help but remember how she and Gavin had raced each other along those very sands, ending with a rock over there. Gavin used to climb the side and swear he could see fantastic creatures in the sea.

"Mermaids," he had laughed, "and a handsome merman. One look like that and he'll splash right out and carry you off!"

So real was the memory of Gavin's banter, so tangible his laughter, that a moment later when she all but fell over a prostrate human form, she couldn't even scream.

Starting with a gasp, she looked down upon a man – quite the most handsome man she had ever seen. A man of ... of gold, for so he seemed with the sunlight gilding his tanned skin, streaking his fair hair and glinting faintly

5

from the yellow sand crusted over his long, powerful limbs. The impression, so close to Gavin's notion about mermen, was so strong that Celia froze for one split second, imagining she had surprised some young sea god asleep.

She came back to reality with a shudder. It's a body, she thought sickly, a body washed up from last night's storm!

The tiniest movement of his ribs drew her back from her horror. He breathed – but just barely. She could see it clearly now, for only a few shreds of fabric clung to him, as if his clothing had been violently ripped away.

Growing bolder, she bent down. His face was caked with salt, his lips cracked and split, his forehead marked at the hairline with what must have been a deep and recent gash. He lay on his stomach, arms outstretched, fingers dug fiercely into the sand, as if he had heaved himself up onto this thin margin of safety with the last of his conscious strength. Celia paused only long enough to take one more look at the thick lashes sealed with sand, and, with a small, jolting cry, sprinted for the farmhouse.

"A half-drowned man," Aunt Meg exclaimed as if Celia had announced a monster of the deep. "Lordy! I'll call Doc Morgan. You and Bart go down and pick him up."

Meg was shooing neighbors off the party line as Celia and her uncle pulled out in the blue

6

pickup truck. They took the track to the shore, Uncle Bart expertly spurting the vehicle over the softest part of the sand to drive along the water's edge. When they came to the motionless body, Celia got the blanket from the cab and Bart let down the backboard. Between them, they got the fellow into the back, where Celia cradled his limp head as the truck picked its way back to the grassy verge. The tiny bedroom off the kitchen was made up and when their charge was safely laid in, Bart peered at him intently.

"Don't know him," he declared, for the old man could recognize just about everybody within a fifty mile radius, "Must be a tourist. Police in town'll know if anybody's missing."

During the hour it took for the doctor to arrive, the man lay utterly still. Except for the tiny, telltale rising of his ribs, he might have been quite dead. Yet Doc Morgan's examination was brief and summary.

"Total exhaustion plus a bit of a knock on the head. Otherwise he's as healthy as a mule. Let him sleep it off and start him on food slowly when he wakes up."

When the stranger had been bathed and tucked into a set of ancient, yellowing pajamas that had once been a Christmas gift Bart refused to wear, the doctor strode out to his dusty green car.

"I'll report this in town," he said. "Somebody's probably worried sick about this guy by now. Beats me how he ever got across those currents to the shore."

After he left, it took some time for the excitement to wear off. But eventually Bart went back to the fields with the hay mower and Meg returned to bottling dill pickles. Celia, with a sigh, picked up her hat and hoe on the way to the large garden at the side of the house.

Lowering her long lashes against the glare of the sun, she threw herself into hoeing the cabbages with the same frantic energy she had applied to everything since the first searing shock of Gavin's death. But this time, she paused to gaze out at the sea which washed up to the bottom of the slope the low grey house was built upon. The water was now so smilingly, so deceptively calm, yet only the night before its screaming winds and lashing waters had been trying to claim another human life for its hungry depths.

"But he made it to shore," Celia murmured, "still alive. I saw him breathe!"

And something very like triumph gleamed in the depths of her clear hazel eyes.

She worked doggedly on, for the garden, the nurture of the thriving green rows, was Celia's major solace, especially on this sad anniversary.

A night and a day and another night passed

before the stranger showed signs of regaining consciousness. Breakfast was barely finished on the third morning when a low moan brought them all dashing to his side. After his long stillness, he tossed about, uttering sharp sounds, as if he had to fight his way to consciousness through some raging inner ocean of his own.

"He's really waking up!" Meg exclaimed excitedly. "I bet the first thing he asks for is a long cool drink!"

She was right. His head rolled, his lashes fluttered and he opened his dry, chapped lips.

"Water,' he whispered thickly. "Please ... water ..."

Aunt Meg was ready. Steadying his head, she held to his lips a china cup brimming coldly from the ever-running spring which fed the house. After the initial awkward taste, he drank thirstily, his eyes closed in bliss as the liquid made its sweet restoring way down his throat.

Celia stood poised at the foot of the bed, watching as he paused after those first hungry gulps to draw breath and look up. With a small intake of air, she saw that his eyes were as golden as the rest of him, a rich amber color flecked with little lights. This gave them the most peculiar intensity as they fixed on the first thing they met – Celia herself – and seemed to drink her in with a wide, half-astonished gaze.

9

A self-conscious flush was beginning to mount her cheeks by the time her aunt turned away to refill the empty cup.

"Here. The doctor said you were to drink your fill."

This time he swallowed slowly, gratefully, but his eyes never wavered from Celia's face. He looked, she thought absurdly, like a saint who was having a vision and didn't quite know what to do about it. When the cup was drained, the man seemed to shake himself a little and gaze about the room.

"Thank you," he managed. "That was ... the most delicious thing I've ever tasted!"

"Humph! T'was only water. I've got some good hot broth on the stove for you."

Moments later Aunt Meg was determinedly spooning the thick, nourishing soup into his mouth. He ate a good deal of it then lay back, apparently revived, upon the pillow.

"Well," said Aunt Meg briskly, "that bit of warm stuff should perk you up. You've been sleeping like an anchor for two days. You gave us a turn, I must say!"

"Two ... days?"

The stranger's brows furrowed uncomprehendingly.

"Why yes. Celia here practically fell right over you lying on the beach. Just made it out of the water, you did. You must have had an

10

accident in the storm."

"Storm?" the man said, as if he had never heard the word before.

"Sure. Fit to capsize the devil. You washed ashore from somewhere and people must be frantic about you. Tell us your name and we'll give your folks a call."

The stranger blinked, wrinkling his forehead in great consternation. His gold eyes became very distant, troubled with an abstraction Celia could not recognize. Then his face went still as he looked from one to the other of the little group.

"I'm afraid I can't tell you my name. I . . . don't remember what it is!"

He said this so calmly that it took a full half-minute for the incredible statement to penetrate. Aunt Meg's hand flew to her mouth.

"But . . . it's your own name! I can understand you being a little confused, but . . ."

"I'm sorry, ma'am," the stranger interposed with the greatest politeness, "but I'm more than a little confused. I don't recall one single thing about who I am or what I'm doing here. I'm trying to make it come, but all I get is . . . a blank!"

"Well, don't push the lad, Meg," Uncle Bart put in quietly. "Poor fellow just darned near drowned. Things'll come back to him soon enough."

11

The stranger seemed glad enough to slip back to sleep, but by lunch time he was wide awake and ready for the bowl of broth Celia brought. He struggled up and took the spoon himself.

"Thanks," he grinned. "This stuff is worth getting half drowned for."

Celia found herself smiling, her eyes attracted for the first time to the thick gold ring on the man's right hand. Two large stones, one of spring-water clarity, the other red as blood, gleamed softly in the subdued light and she couldn't help but think it was a rather gaudy thing for a man to be wearing. It also reminded her how she had found him wearing little else – and she blushed.

By supper time their guest was well enough to take a complete tray. He ate and drank heartily, flashing a grateful white smile between courses. It was as if his body, like some powerful machine strained to the point of breakdown, was now shaking itself vigorously back to life.

"Now," said Bart affably after the peaches and custard had been tucked away, "how's the memory getting on? Any more recollection of who you are?"

The stranger shook his fair, sun-streaked head.

"No. Can't get a blessed thing to come back

to me."

His voice, having found its natural timbre, sent a rich masculine vibration through the room, compelling attention. The heavy ring flashed in the slanting evening sun and the three listeners felt a strange inability to press him further until Doc Morgan arrived in the morning to take charge of this puzzling matter.

The grizzled doctor spent an eternity closeted in the bedroom, then shrugged at the three people waiting expectantly in the kitchen.

"I guess it's amnesia," he sighed. "With the strain the fellow's been under, it's quite possible."

Uncle Bart looked perplexed. Unidentified strangers weren't his usual run of difficulty.

"Isn't anybody in town looking for him?"

"Nope. Even the police haven't heard a thing."

"Well ... how long before he remembers who he is?"

Doc Morgan moved his shoulders.

"Can't say. A few hours, a few days, maybe never. I can take him off your hands if he's going to be a problem. You folks have done more than enough as is."

Uncle Bart wouldn't hear of it.

"We found him and we'll look after him till he gets his bearings. He's no bother at all."

The doctor nodded wordlessly. In this

13

sparsely populated corner of the province, hospitality still ran strong. He hadn't expected Bart to release his castaway.

"Suit yourself. Only don't go pushing him to remember. If he keeps trying and can't it'll only make things worse. Leave him be and he'll come to himself in his own good time."

Celia, with more life than she had felt in months, followed the brisk man back to his car.

"What causes amnesia?" she asked curiously. "I've only seen it mentioned once or twice in books."

The doctor rubbed his forehead slowly.

"It's still a bit of a mystery. It can occur because of a bump on the head. Or it can happen when people get so fed up with their lives they decide to block the past right out and start all over again somewhere else. Those are the types that go to the corner for a quart of milk and disappear. Some of them never remember where they came from."

"And ... and the man we found?"

"I couldn't say, girl." The doctor slammed the door. "I just couldn't say."

Pensively, Celia watched until the car swung out of sight behind the ash trees. Then she walked back to the house to find the stranger sitting up in bed, his tawny eyes cheerful and alert.

"I'm about ready to get up now, if ... um, I

14

just had something to put on."

Aunt Meg measured him with her eyes.

"Well, you're quite a bit bigger than Bart, but I'll see what I can do."

It was lucky Bart liked his clothing baggy. After much searching, the stranger was outfitted in a nut-brown work shirt so strained at the shoulders it left a broad, open V of wiry hair, as golden as the rest of him, down the front. For bottoms, he got the loan of some striped blue overalls, much faded from the wash, and more than a trifle too short in the leg.

Foot gear was harder, but finally he was strapped into a pair of ancient sandals that promised not to pinch too much when he walked. This outlandish get-up seemed to delight the stranger and his smile shed a wordless, merry brightness in the room.

"I'll get you something cool to drink," Celia said, trying to hide her astonishment at how tall he was, "and you can just sit out on the porch. It's not too hot in the shade."

He strode behind her easily, the only traces of his ordeal being the fading cut at his hairline and a certain added keenness to his high, bold cheekbones.

Settling him in a weatherbeaten wicker rocker, Celia found herself oddly tongue-tied by this new, very male, presence. Quickly, she

15

took up her hat and hoe for a fresh attack on the unrelenting weeds in the garden.

As soon as she stepped out, the July sun laid itself across her back like a broad, hot palm, making her sleeveless yellow top cling silkily to her skin as she moved. She bent down, but her usual concentration escaped her. Like a wary forest creature, an instinct told her she was being watched. She didn't hear the quiet footfalls, however, until the stranger was directly behind her.

"Oh," she started nervously, "I didn't know you were there."

Tawny eyes, so flecked with sun they seemed lit from within, took in the pretty oval face and the shining tumble of hair that framed it.

"Sorry. I just wondered if I could give you a hand."

"Oh goodness no." Her inexplicable flush rose again. "Not after just getting out of a sick bed. I wouldn't think of it!"

Instead of returning to his chair, the man watched in silence as Celia pulled up ragweed by the root. A moment later he took over the row opposite and set to work. In about two minutes, Celia noticed what he was doing and let out a small gasp of distress.

"My little sage plants!" she half whispered. "You're pulling them out!"

"Oh ... I'm sorry. I didn't ... I thought

16

they were weeds. I'm afraid I'm not very familiar with gardening."

"It's all right." Celia hastened to cover her chagrin at seeing her little herbs lying helpless in the sun. "I'll just stick them right in again and they won't be any the worse."

Digging in the damp earth with her fingers, she set each displaced plant upright again, releasing as she did so a silent prayer for its survival. The stranger followed her movements intently.

"You're as tender of them as if they were children."

"If you're determined to help, I better give you a guided tour so you can pick out the culprits and leave the good guys alone," Celia said with a smile.

The chance to show off her garden soon brought animation to Celia's face. Corn, chard, watermelons, and tomatoes were all pointed out with equal pride. A bemused quirk touched her lips at the stranger's avid interest, as if he were trying to fix each new leaf and stem firmly in his memory. Celia indicated an overloaded row along the fence.

"Try the blackberries. I like them best straight off the bush."

Strong white teeth crushed the juice from the glossy fruit, and stained lips curved into a smile.

"Delicious! I didn't know a simple handful of berries could be so good."

His pleasure was so obvious that Celia had to smile back and let him hoe among the carrots until it was time to bring in the cows. Despite her worried protests, the stranger started out at her side.

"The only thing wrong with me is some mighty sore muscles in my back. And this terrific sea air has made me forget about them already."

Celia hopped down the bank to her shortcut along the shore and the stranger followed nimbly, taking great bracing breaths of the salt breeze. He kept pace easily, making scarcely a sound in the soft sand except for the awkward flap of the ill-fitting sandals. But when they reached the trampled area beside the truck tracks, he stopped abruptly.

"So this is where you found me, washed up just like a piece of driftwood."

Celia nodded, pushing a soft tendril back from her forehead. The small diamond ring she still cherished tenderly made a spark of white fire in the sun and caught the stranger's eye.

"Finders keepers," he grinned. "I think that's how it goes. Only I don't know what your fellow is going to say when he finds you keeping a mixed up castaway in your back yard."

18

"I ... I don't have a fellow," responded Celia quietly. "My fiance was killed two years ago."

She could not tell whether it was a fleeting touch she felt upon her shoulder or not. But when she had composed herself enough to face him, the stranger was staring out at the treacherous waves, his features enigmatically stilled in a chiselled mask.

"I'm sorry," he said simply. "I didn't know."

Immediately Celia knew he wouldn't foist upon her any of those horrid platitudes so many people ladle out to the bereaved. Grateful for his delicacy of feeling, she began to walk on. They continued in silence along the curve of the beach until they reached the path to the pasture.

The placid holsteins, chewing their cuds like matrons gossiping at tea, set off toward the lane at the mere sight of Celia. But as the pair approached to open the gate, one broad-beamed beauty snuffed loudly at the stranger's elbow. A long purple tongue flicked out, making him jump back with such confused surprise that Celia stifled a giggle.

"Don't worry. She's just trying to find out what you're all about."

"If she can find that out," the man laughed, "I'd be very grateful myself."

19

He extended a hand toward the inquisitive beast, and Celia noticed for the first time how broad his palm was, promising great strength. Yet the skin gleamed, uncalloused, almost silken smooth, and the nails had been expertly manicured not a very great while before.

All the way back to the barn the stranger walked behind the cows with the air of a small boy being allowed close to them for the first time. Delightedly, he watched as each beast found her stanchion, drawn by the waiting treat of dairy ration. When he wondered why the stable wasn't full, Bart, washing the udders and hauling out the ancient milking machine, shook his head.

"Used to have a bigger herd but I'm getting too old for the work. Besides, the price of milk isn't going up. Next year I'm selling off the lot and likely the farm as well."

"Then you have no . . . er, son to take over for you?"

"Nope," Bart snorted. "And it wouldn't make any difference if I did. He'd just have taken off for the city like every other young sprout from these parts. Nothin' to keep 'em down on the farm."

Celia hurried to feed the calves. She hated it when Uncle Bart talked of selling, although she knew it was inevitable. There was no one to carry on. Aunt Meg and he would probably get

20

a house in town where they would mope for the sight of the sea and their own beloved fields. Celia would get a job in some office just when she had discovered how much she loved, how much she needed, the land she had grown up on. Oh well.

Pails clattered as the stranger asked Bart why. The old man deftly attached a milker cup that had been scrubbed spotless by Celia in the morning.

"Times have changed. The small farm can't make it any more – can't compete with city wages. I never had the money to expand, though lord knows there's land going idle all around here. Big investors buy it up, you know. They let it run to brambles while they sit in some plush office waiting to make a kill on the market."

"But ... a farm could be made to pay?"

"Oh sure. All you need is money and brains and muscle. Me, I've had my day. I'm just looking for a nice little place to retire."

The tall, golden-eyed man watched, sunk in thought, as Bart's gnarled hands stripped the last milk from each cow. He helped carry the frothing pails to the cooler and, when the last utensil had been scoured and the cows turned out for the night, the threesome went to the house where a rich, beefy aroma greeted them. Savory meat chunks floating in gravy filled the great tureen on the table. With the gusto of a half-starved man, the stranger dug in.

"This is terrific," he exclaimed. "You wouldn't get anything as good in the fanciest restaurant."

Aunt Meg became happily flustered.

"Oh now, I expect it's the beef. Home-grown makes a difference. We raise a little one for the freezer every year."

After dinner the stranger refused to go directly to bed, even though a faint shadow of fatigue showed around his amber eyes. He followed them out onto the veranda where Aunt Meg crocheted and Bart peered at the paper. Celia sat on the steps, absently watching the sun sink toward the molten horizon. Their guest cleared his throat to attract the attention of the old farmer.

"I'd like to work for you, Mr. Walton, if you don't mind. You've been kind enough to take me in and ... well, I want to make myself as useful as I can."

Bart looked up, surprised.

"Oh, you don't have to put yourself out any. Besides, the wages I could offer wouldn't tempt a school kid."

"I certainly wouldn't expect to be paid!" The stranger actually seemed close to a blushing. "Nothing I could do could make up for the generosity you've already shown me, and you'll

have to teach me from scratch anyway. I'd ...
like to stay until I get things ... straightened
out, though naturally I'd hate to be a nuisance.
I could easily move on if..."

"Nonsense! We wouldn't think of letting you
go," Aunt Meg declared. "Not with you in a
muddle and not even having a shirt to your
back. Haying's started and we're darned glad
for all the help we can get."

Bart agreed, but Celia could see the irony in
his eyes as he was torn between the sight of the
soft smooth hands, obviously unacquainted
with physical labor, and approval of the broad
powerful back that promised an easy way with
the hundreds of bales soon to go into the hay
loft. Help was all but impossible to get. Bart
had planned to muddle through this last year as
best he could. Assistance from this stranger
would be a stroke of luck – providing he could
be kept from injuring himself in the machinery
or the aches and blisters didn't send him
high-tailing it to the nearest town in search of a
more civilized way to earn his keep.

"Thanks a lot." A happy smile lit the
stranger's face. "I'll do my best. I promise."

Later, when the fading of the day sent them
all to bed, Celia paused in her quiet seaward
room to listen to the slap of the waves upon the
shore. This was the hour she was most
vulnerable, when solitude and darkness made

her think most often of Gavin. But for once, the lapping of the water failed to make her shudder. On impulse, she opened the window to let in the salt air and the light of the rising moon.

She stood for a moment, palely abstracted, wondering about the mysterious golden stranger who had been washed into their lives. Who was he? Where did he come from? Why did no one care enough to clamor over half the country the fact that he was missing?

Her smooth forehead knitted, but no answers came. With a sigh, she slipped into the huge old bed, her slim figure curled up in its expanse more like a weary child falling innocently to sleep than a grown woman already battered by one of life's bitterest blows.

CHAPTER TWO

In the morning, the stranger offered to go for the cows by himself, but Celia went along to show him the secrets of the stubborn creaking gates. Well before breakfast, when the mist, like the scarves of dreaming dancers, floated toward the sea, they took the path uphill to where the cattle lay fast asleep.

"Seems a shame," the stranger's eyes crinkled, "to get the poor ladies up. They sure could use their beauty sleep."

From Celia came the rarest of sounds, the chime of laughter. He had a sense of humor, this man. What other delicious qualities lay under that handsome exterior?

"Don't worry. They appreciate being milked. If we let them sleep they'd be mooing at the gate by noon."

Impishness was surfacing in Celia, the same trait that had captivated Gavin so long ago. The pair circled until each cow heaved herself to her feet and started over the dew-shiny grass. Celia pulled the awkward old gate behind them, grimacing as it protested every inch on screeching hinges.

"Make sure it's hooked with this pesky bit of wire," she said, "or it'll swing open by itself and let the cows into Archy Hope's corn next door. Then you'll be able to hear Archy roaring in the next county!"

In the barn, the stranger learned how to attach the milker and scrub out all the utensils. There was, however, considerable chuckling when he tried to strip the last milk from the cow by hand. No way could he get the strong white stream to flow the way Bart could.

"It's your hands, son," Bart grinned. "Takes you at least a week to get the feel of it."

25

The stranger sighed good humoredly at his own smooth knuckles where gleamed that incongruous ring.

"Yeah, guess so. I'll just have to take a crack at something else!"

Picking up the broad old shovel, he went to work on the cement gutters after the cows had left. He worked with a will, though once, standing with the odor of the barnyard reeking around him, he flung back his fine profile in a merry laugh.

"I can't for the life of me tell why," he chuckled to Celia who was looking at him over an armful of yellow straw for the calves, "but there seems to be something screamingly funny about me pitching in on a job like this."

"Well, everyone has to start at the bottom and work up." Celia pointed to the cavernous mow above, "We will be tossing bales around in there when it's ninety-nine in the shade."

The stranger finished carefully, casting an eye behind him to see that the gutter was spotless and that the shovel, clean and dry, was where he had found it. The three went to the house where an enormous breakfast of bacon and eggs, oatmeal and coffee waited on the stove.

"You need your strength on a farm," said Aunt Meg, ladling out porridge. "Breakfast is what keeps you going the rest of the day."

Afterwards, the stranger went with Bart on the tractor to the upper meadow where the hay was ready to be raked. Celia picked up her hoe and headed for the large potato patch behind the driveshed. The rows needed hilling, the pigweed was gaining ground and a hungry vanguard of Colorado potato beetles was already eating its way through the plants.

Tilting her straw hat against the sun, she worked steadily until lunchtime when she went to help her aunt set out green pea soup, cold roast beef, a salad that had been growing in the garden not an hour before, thick slabs of home-baked bread, and the strong brown tea so beloved by country folks. There was milk and coffee and the stranger drank his share. But in the middle of the meal he took a pitcher to the spring and brought it back brimming full.

"The water tastes so fine here," he said, downing a glass. "It's better than any wine."

The blank faces of Bart and Meg showed they knew nothing about wine. The stranger, Celia thought, apparently did.

They ate until Aunt Meg, having asked for the butter, the sugar, and the bread to be passed, threw up her hands.

"This is ridiculous," she said to the stranger. "If you're going to stay here, we can't just keep saying 'hey you'. We'll have to give you a name."

The stranger took another swallow of spring water and turned to Celia with a twinkle in his eyes.

"Your aunt is right. I do need a name. What do you think I should be called?"

"Why ... I don't know. What name would you like?"

"I'd like the name you give me. You'll never get a chance to name a full-grown man again."

Yes, she thought a full-grown man tossed at her feet, a caprice of the waves, a new-born god opening his eyes to life.

"I think ... I think I'll call you Adam!" she said suddenly.

"Adam," the stranger mused. "The first man. I like that."

For some inexplicable reason, Celia felt herself go pink.

"It's just ... the first thing that came into my head. After all, you must have a perfectly good name of your own."

"True," he grinned, "but since I don't know what it is, Adam will suit me just fine."

For someone at a loss about himself, the man showed amazingly little concern about his own past life.

Celia worked among the potatoes all afternoon, her slender figure moving rhythmically in her faded blue jeans and sunflower yellow top, heaping crumbly reddish soil with her hoe, bending down to pull the weeds, lifting a green branch to examine it for insect damage. When the drone of the returning tractor told her it was time to quit, she saw with surprise that Adam was driving and her uncle hanging onto the seat behind. Adam waved gaily.

"He let me drive," he called, delightedly. "I even had a crack at raking hay."

That was something. Ordinarily the only people Uncle Bart let touch his tractor were herself and Aunt Meg, in a pinch.

"He's not half bad on the rake," Bart admitted. "After he got himself tangled up a few times he got the hang of it. Might make a farmer of the fellow yet!"

Celia smiled at this high praise. It took skill to wheel the big side-delivery rake around the field and have it turn out neat, evenly spaced windrows of hay instead of lumpy crooked tangles that would choke the baler and make Bart swear later on.

Three more days passed, in which Adam worked steadfastly beside Bart and showed not the least sign of remembering who he was. Doc Morgan stopped by to declare him in perfect health except for this strange lapse of memory.

"You know," he said to Adam, "seems like this amnesia thing is going to hang on for a bit. Best thing for you to do is drop in at the police station in town. They'll take your picture and connect you up with missing persons files across the county and maybe the States, too. Could be somebody, somewhere, will recognize you."

Adam shrugged as if it made no difference one way or the other. But the next day, he climbed into the pickup truck with Bart and headed into town. At lunch time, when they returned, Adam stepped down, resplendent in new blue jeans and a fawn coloured shirt which, though inexpensive and workmanlike, had been chosen with a very discerning eye. Never before had the broadness of his shoulders, the narrowness of his hips, or the power of his strong, corded arms been shown to such advantage.

A wide belt and squeaky new leather boots completed the outfit and a large package under his arm promised more changes of clothes.

"Your uncle has been treating me. Now I look as if I belong around here."

When Adam went into the small bedroom to put aside his purchases, Aunt Meg looked at Bart.

"Did you go the police?"

"Yep. Sergeant Hazlitt took quite an interest. Took pictures and asked enough questions for three people. Told me on the sly that they got to keep a real eye out for smugglers on the coast. They're at it now as much as they ever were."

Everybody knew that. In the old days it had been slaves spirited to freedom, arms slipped to beleaguered loyalists, rumrunning during Prohibition. Now more sinister cargoes – drugs, diamonds, and gangland bosses – slipped daringly past borders in the fastest of yachts.

"Humph!' Meg snorted. "Our Adam wouldn't be mixed up in anything like that!"

If Adam noticed how the conversation lagged when he entered the room, he never showed it. Pausing for a drink of spring water, he ran his hand through his hair. The flashy ring glittered in the noon sun. Celia, unable to keep her eyes away from it, wondered for the dozenth time where Adam would get such a thing and why he would wear it. But then, she was a country girl not used to seeing the calloused hands around her wearing any more adornment than a battered wedding band, too tight to pull off for the heavy work.

Late that afternoon, Celia went to pick some fresh raspberries for dessert. They would go well with the ice cream her uncle had brought back, and had to be picked before the robins ate them all. She hoped Adam liked raspberries and ice cream. They had been Gavin's favorite. Two summers ago he had come with her to this very spot and had blown little kisses along the side of her neck as she reached among the prickly bushes.

"Oh Gavin," she whispered, as once more her thoughts returned to the love she had shared with him.

Sadly, she began to pick the plump fruit, not caring that she tore her fine skin on the small, wicked thorns or that her hands were soon a welter of scarlet scratches.

Soon her pail was full and her skin was smarting up to her wrists. When she took the pail into the kitchen, Aunt Meg, looking at Celia's scratched hands shook her greying head. But before she could say anything, the screen door squeaked open and in sprang Adam, an enormous fragrant bunch of wild honeysuckle, black-eyed Susans, blue devil, and white clover in his arms.

"Flowers for the ladies!" he cried. "These were so beautiful by the lane, I thought we ought to have an armful for the house."

Celia found herself choking on a giggle and Aunt Meg looked thoroughly startled. Apparently Adam didn't know that no true-bred countryman would be caught dead picking flowers – especially if those flowers normally came under the classification of weeds!

"They're lovely," Celia smiled, as the blue

petals, pink bells, and gay white stars were arranged in a vase. "We . . . haven't had flowers in the house for ages."

He never suspected a thing as the two of them went off to start the milking. Adam could now handle the milkers easily, taking pail after pail to the cooler. In fearless trust, he stood within range of the great splayed hooves.

"They must be getting to like me," he put in cheerfully, "I haven't had a single hostile move yet."

"Oh don't worry," Celia smiled. "Every one of them knows who's friendly and who isn't."

After dinner, Adam followed Celia to the potato patch where she explained that she had to wait for the stillness and the dew of evening to dust the leaves against the depredations of the potato beetle. Adam examined a few leaves already gnawed down to their stalks.

"They sure are hungry. Do you have this problem every year?"

"Oh yes. And it's much worse on those big farms that grow nothing but potatoes."

"Imagine that," exclaimed Adam. "All those city people eat potatoes every day – and they haven't the least idea of the trouble it takes to grow them. We take a lot for granted, I guess."

They had made lemonade on the porch, and Adam started asking about who the people were around there and where they came from.

He seemed to be trying to make himself into a giant sponge, soaking up all the information to be had. Celia spoke of succeeding waves of settlers and mentioned the Acadian French, who had been considered such a security threat by the British that they had been forcibly uprooted from their homes and scattered across the continent.

"There's the story of Evangeline, who was separated from her sweetheart in the move and spent the rest of her life trying to find him."

"Did she ever see him again?"

"Oh yes, but only when he was old and dying in a poorhouse. Evangeline herself died of grief a short time later. It's such a . . . lovely tale of real devotion."

Adam took his amber eyes off the reddening sea to look at Celia.

"It certainly is . . . but don't you think they were a bit foolish, wasting their whole lives when they might have been happy with somebody else?"

Celia stiffened. Who was this fellow to criticize the most beautiful of the Nova Scotian folk tales!

"Some people love only once," she said, her face turning away so swiftly that Adam could only see the gilding of the sunset on her glossy curls, "and . . . forever. Nothing can change it."

"Not even . . . death?"

Though his voice was gentle, a rush of wild resentment swept through the girl at his side. How dare he hint, like Aunt Meg and everybody else, that a person could just sweep out the pains of the heart like some kind of spring cleaning, if only one set one's mind to it. She had loved Gavin, loved him with her life. Didn't anybody understand that?

She stood up and brushed a tress away from her agitated face.

"The mosquitoes are coming out," she said tightly. "I think it's time I went to bed."

Leaving Adam gazing after her, she hurried up the stairs to her silent room.

She slipped into her nightgown and under the sheets, but sleep eluded her. Instead, Evangeline on her sorrowful quest, interchanged with Gavin's lost face, swirled through her mind. Was this to haunt her for the rest of her days? Was it?

Suddenly, she found her heart rebelling.

"Forever!" She whispered the word in the darkness and heard such a dismal lonely sound that she shivered inside. To be forever without love, to live with nothing but memories for the rest of her life.

Twice during the night she was driven to switch on her lamp and pace the floor. At other times she had simply mourned the past. Now

35

she agonized over a future that stretched desperately empty before her, if all she had to fill it was the memory of Gavin.

Her heart ached. She buried her face in her slender, sun-browned hands. For the first time since Gavin had disappeared she felt she must demand more of life than this eternal misery of grief.

The next day Celia took the morning to pick green beans. This would be her last chance to work on her own for quite a while. After lunch her uncle intended to bring out the ancient baler and start baling the hay. From then on there would be scarcely a break until the barn was filled to the rafters with sweet smelling winter rations for the dairy cows.

"We'll start on the upper meadow today," Bart had told them. "Tomorrow maybe we can get the elevator up and bring a few loads in."

After lunch, it took over an hour to thread baling twine into the machine and smooth its cantankerous temper into working order after a year of idleness in the musty machine shed. Celia went along as a matter of course, for she always drove the tractor which powered the baler while her uncle rode the little two-wheeled stacker trailing behind. His job was to lift the bales from the back of the baler, stack them in a little pyramid of six on a platform behind him and then, by pulling a lever, let the platform drop so that the pile of bales was deposited neatly on the stubble. From there, a big hay fork could scoop them up and deposit them on the wagon later on.

"Take her easy for a while," Bart yelled over the thundering machine. "Got to work the rust out of her and make sure she's tyin' decent knots."

Slowly they started around the field, Celia guiding the big tractor with one eye while keeping the other critically on the windrow of hay being picked up and fed into the maw of the baler. Once there, a powerful packer and wicked cutting knives transformed it into a dense, oblong, tidy bale.

Adam watched from the shade of a butternut tree while Celia, skillfully changing from low to second, and then to third gear, coaxed the baler around the field with only one or two temperamental hitches. He did not stay under the tree for long. Next time Celia looked, Adam was riding the stacker and Uncle Bart stood under the butternut tree. He did not stand for long. Unable to endure idleness, he shooed Celia off the tractor and took over the driving himself.

"You might as well go home and help your Aunt Meg. Adam's pretty handy on that stacker."

Celia, who liked to drive the thundering train

of machinery, nevertheless yielded up her place with a sigh of relief. She was only too glad to see her uncle at ease on the tractor seat while a younger man took on the hard, heavy job of wrestling bales out of the stream of dust and chaff.

By the time the two of them returned, dust-encrusted and sunburned, Celia had the cows in their stanchions, udders all washed down and ready. Familiar with the routine now, Adam got out the milking machines and attached them to the first cow without being told. Uncle Bart leaned against a glossy flank approvingly.

"Got the whole field ready to bring in," he told his niece. "Adam's pretty good on that stacker."

Celia looked at Adam, a rare smile touching her lips.

"You better watch it," she warned. "You might wake some morning with your arms a foot longer than they were when you started."

Adam flashed a grin and rubbed his shoulder.

"I can believe it. If it gets too bad, I can always donate myself to the zoo."

Though he was smiling, Celia noticed that his hands were covered with blisters, some of which had been bleeding. Meekly, he let her examine them.

"Look at that," she scolded. "I'll fix these up tonight and tomorrow you wear gloves. You're not made out of harness leather like Uncle Bart."

In the house, he allowed her to pour disinfectant on his sores. Instead of wincing, he sat with a small smile on his lips – which caused Meg and Bart to exchange a glance.

"Best nurse in the country," Adam kidded, and Celia was astonished to find herself going quite pink in the cheeks.

The next morning was spent in bolting together the long, ladder-like hay elevator and hoisting its end up through the small door high under the eaves of the barn. The toothed chain, which was driven by a small electric motor, would carry the bales from the wagon up into the stifling mow where some hardy soul would have to brave the trapped heat while stacking the bales in long rows the length of the barn.

Adam moved gingerly, giving away the soreness that the sudden strenuous work had inflicted upon his surprised muscles. Yet he neither complained nor listened to Celia's warnings to slow down for a while.

"It's just great," he grinned, heaving powerfully at the end of the elevator while Bart, high in the barn, secured the other end with a chain, "to get my body active like this. Who cares about a couple of aches and pains!"

The strong outlines of his shoulders rippled and strained against his shirt as he worked to keep the elevator steady. Unable to help herself, Celia ran her eyes along the broad, muscle-corded back so thinly disguised by the fabric – and felt a queer butterfly tremor ripple through her insides.

She turned away, heat prickling into her cheeks. She knew the feeling well – knew that for the first time since Gavin's death she had looked at a man with open admiration in her eyes.

Well, she thought, thankful that Adam's attention was on Bart's signals, he certainly is good looking. Any girl would have to grant him that.

But it wasn't just "any girl". It was herself, the heartbroken mourner, supposedly shut off from men for all time.

Oh Gavin, her soul cried out suddenly, Gavin, my darling!

But Gavin's face would not come to her, clear and distinct, as it always had before. It was blurred, distant, as if a fine gauzy veil had been slipped over it when she hadn't been looking. Closing her eyes, she tried hard, but the veil refused to slide away.

And that was how, at last, she knew that she was losing him.

At lunch Celia was disturbingly aware of

Adam. She noticed, as never before, the crisply mannered way in which he handled the cutlery, the way he closed his long-lashed eyes each time he tasted the spring water he insisted on having beside him at every meal. She saw that his tan was deepening into a rich bronze glow of health. His hair, though merrily windblown, was wonderfully wavy and had most certainly been shaped by one of those expensive men's hair stylists that cater to the very rich. Whoever he was, this enigmatic man of gold had not stepped out of any rough background.

Pensively, Celia pulled weeds from among her cucumber vines while the men fitted the hay fork to the loader on the bigger of the two tractors and repaired the racks of the hay wagon. Unaccustomed thoughts flitted through her mind. Time sped by, and before she knew it, she had to dash along the shore to bring home the cows.

Adam worked happily at her side during the milking chores, laughing and cracking little jokes. After dinner, he joined her as she sat on the grass under the peaceful shade of the maple.

From the way he sprawled out she could see that he had acquired a whole new perception of what it meant to rest. He lay gazing out over the sun-dappled seat and listening to the cry of the gulls as they wheeled overhead.

"I saw a lot of those birds hanging about inland," he mused. "I thought they did all their hunting over water."

Celia laughed.

"Oh they love farms. They're always behind the plow to see what they can pick up. There are all kinds of easy snacks when hay is cut, I suppose."

Adam followed the free, swooping flights for a while with his eyes. Then he rolled over on his back and wanted to know who all the neighbors were and what they did. And when that had been gone through, he asked what it was like out here in the winter and what happened to all the milk after the shining tank truck picked it up in the morning.

"Goodness," Celia declared, "aren't you trying to find out everything all at once? I haven't heard so many questions since exam day at school."

She was glad to tell him what she knew – glad to speak of impersonal things. How easy it was to sit and talk to this stranger. He had no past and that made it seem as if she had no past either. There was only the present and the future, and none of the perilous pitfalls a foray into her immediate history would have brought.

At night now, Celia had begun to sleep much better. Whether this could be attributed to lessening grief or just plain old-fashioned weariness, she couldn't tell, for they had just now begun the most strenuous task of the year.

With the addition of Adam, the three blended into a well-matched team. Celia drove the tractor which pulled the hay wagon from stack to small stack. Adam got command of the bigger tractor with the hay fork, which he was supposed to slide in under the pyramids of six and jockey up on the loader to the wagon. Uncle Bart worked on the hay wagon, taking bales the loader had set down and packing them neatly into a wagonload.

The first morning was slow. Adam, unused to the operation of the loader, missed with the six-pronged fork as many times as he hit, knocking the little pyramids to the ground.

"Hey," Bart joked, "put 'em up by hand. Might be faster. Maybe you're a city slicker after all!"

Adam grinned, hopping down to reconstruct the latest pile he had knocked over.

"Oh just you wait. I'll get the hang of it yet!"

With a great deal of banter, they watched while Adam developed an understanding with his machine. Deliberately, he clowned a little so that Celia, from her perch, let out the first completely free peal of laughter that had been heard from her since Gavin died. Adam glowed with delight. Uncle Bart, though he said

43

nothing, let his old face crinkle into a wreath of smiles that seemed to say, "Bless you, Adam, and welcome, just for the light you've put back in our Celia's eyes!"

When they reached the barn, Celia carefully pulled the heavily loaded wagon up beside the small wooden platform supporting the end of the elevator.

"You and Adam start unloading," Bart told them. "I'll go up in the mow and see how they fall. Get the stacking started right."

Celia produced her gardening gloves and a pair of tough leather gauntlets for Adam. Ruefully, he looked at his palms. They were still soft.

"I haven't got a decent callus to my name."

"Ha! Stick around here for a week. You'll get your share."

Nimbly, she climbed to the top of the load while Adam heaved a few bales onto the clattering elevator. Celia began lifting hay from the top of the load and shoving it over to where Adam could get a grip. Watching her, his face filled with discomfort.

"You don't have to do that, you know. It isn't ... uh, women's work."

Celia let out a second burst of laughter.

"You don't know much about the country. Around a farm anything is anybody's work who can do it. Usually I unload this wagon by

44

myself."

Disbelief crossed Adam's face as he saw her slender form outlined against the sun. Like most men who were accustomed to thinking of women as fragile, he had little idea of the strength latent in her slim body. Yet only a couple of generations back, her foremothers had uprooted trees and guided plows among the stumps while their husbands served in the king's militia.

"Here," Celia said, and tossed him a heavy bale. "Uncle Bart will be wondering if we're sleeping in the shade."

The enormous load shrank quickly as Celia and Adam fell into a steady give and take rhythm. In a moment a natural, effortless partnership had established itself between them as the work made them forget all but the moving of muscles and the shifting of the dense, sweet smelling hay. It had been the kind of work Celia had sought often before, work that could numb a mind and drive a body until it ached. Only now, instead of trying to drug herself with it, she found herself savoring the other side of it – the joy, the accomplishment, the delight of youth in its own strength and speed and skill.

When they finished, it was near lunchtime. Adam mopped his brow and hopped down from the wagon.

"Hot work!" He, like Celia, was festooned with wisps of yellow hay. "I better get us a little refreshment."

A moment later he was back with a battered dipper that came from the springhouse. It brimmed with clear cold water. He made an elaborate mock bow.

"Care to partake first, milady?"

Celia closed her eyes, letting the heavenly coolness trickle down her throat, tasting – as she had not tasted for months – the sweetness of the spring water. How was it, she wondered, that just being near this smiling stranger could make her want to relish life again?

"Thanks," she murmured. She handed him the dipper, still half full. "Nothing like cold water when the weather's hot."

Adam nodded as he finished off what was left with a single blissful gulp. When he took the dipper away, Celia saw – with a small intaking of breath – that he had drunk deliberately from the exact spot her own parched lips had touched.

For the next two days they worked steadily, finding their own private rhythm, giving themselves up to the dusty, seemingly endless task. Adam and Celia joked back and forth. Uncle Bart watched, only his delighted eyes showing how glad he was.

Celia herself floated in a pleasant state in

which the pain of her loss drifted farther away from her, becoming gradually unreal. No longer did she wake in the night, no longer could a sudden reminder stab at her heart. Whether or not this was simply the healing power of time taking hold at last, she could not tell. She did not try. This new peace, this miraculous lifting of the spirits, was too precious a gift to risk in any crude attempts at analysis.

On the third day, just as the afternoon was at its peak, the big tractor gave a wheeze and sputtered to a halt. Uncle Bart peered into its innards, then straightened, wiping his oily hands.

"Fuel line's busted. Have to get a new piece in town."

"I'll drive in," Celia volunteered. "Just write down what I'm supposed to ask for."

Uncle Bart took on a somewhat sly look.

"Sure, good idea. Take Adam with you and show him around. Day's shot anyway. Drop in at the police station for news. Take yourselves out for a restaurant meal. Change'd do both of you good."

Celia and Adam found themselves grinning at each other like two kids playing hookey. Adam cast a look at the field still dotted with bales, then hesitated.

"Go on," Bart waved them away. "I could

47

use a bit of rest too, you know."

Aunt Meg, with her mouth in a wry line, refused their polite invitation to come along to shop. She dashed off a small list, instead.

"Just pick up a couple of things at Jackon's Supermarket. Won't take you but a minute."

As Celia trotted off to shower the chaff from her skin, she was astonished to hear an almost forgotten sound – herself humming. She actually looked into her wardrobe with interest, searching for something pretty.

She chose a gay pink cotton dress embroidered with rosebuds at the neck. Her hair, still a damp mass of curls from the shower, she bound with the blue iridescence of an Indian scarf.

Goodness, she giggled to herself as she applied a shading of smoky shadow around her shining eyes, you'd think I were some teenager getting myself up for a Saturday afternoon sock hop.

The soft cling of the dress after the ruggedness of her denim jeans and the healthy glow of days in the sun heightened by the unusual dash of make-up made her look so much the enchanting *gamine* that Adam stared in open astonishment as she came out the front door.

"Heavens! Can this be the same strapping country lass who was tossing bales only this morning?"

Celia laughed.

"Women have many disguises. Surely you discovered that when you were about twelve."

Adam gave her a mysterious, good-humored shrug and climbed into the cab of the pickup truck.

"I'll have to drive," Celia said. "You haven't much to show by way of a driver's license."

With toe-tapping country music strumming out of the radio and spirits high, they bumped off down the lane and onto the gravel road to Harristown.

The town drowsed in the afternoon heat. But after they had been to the equipment dealer and the supermarket, it began to stir with suppertime activity. Celia parked the truck on a shady side street lined with high-gabled Victorian houses. The local police station was just at the corner.

"We'd better see," she said, "if anyone has figured out who you are yet."

Adam shrugged again, conveying the impression that his real identity wasn't really of that much interest. He needn't have worried. Sergeant Hazlitt looked up from his cluttered desk and shook his head.

"Haven't heard a peep yet. Let you know when I do."

Outside, the heat of the day was abating.

49

Adam offered Celia his arm. The two of them strolled down the street as grandly as the ladies and gentlemen who had once inhabited the tall gingerbread houses around them. Adam's tall form drew inquiring glances. He was not recognized as a local, yet his outdoor tan and workmanlike clothes declared that he was certainly something more than a tourist passing through.

"Well," he drawled finally, "how about recommending a restaurant where a guy can take a pretty girl for a night on the town."

Celia flushed.

"Uh . . . there's one place. Gaspard's. He got sick of retirement and opened a little nook a couple of years ago. People around here think he's odd but they say he used to be quite a top chef in his day."

"Then Gaspard's it is. Lead on!"

Two streets later they found themselves in front of a very small, very old stone house, now converted into a restaurant. Inside, a low ceilinged room held less than half a dozen tables, but each was resplendent with a snowy white linen table cloth. Hand hewn beams crossed above their heads. A wide stone fireplace looked large enough to roast half an ox.

"Delightful!" Adam cried. "Why isn't it packed at this time of day?"

Celia spread her hands as Adam seated her at a table overlooking a tiny, enclosed rose garden.

"Oh, you know small towns. Locals all stick to the places they're used to."

At that moment a small rotund man bustled out of a door at the back. His drooping grey-flecked moustache bore a vaguely optimistic air, yet also conveyed that he was resigned to disappointment. He greeted them effusively with an engraved menu much too impressive for the charming little place he ran.

"The wine list," he cast a hesitant look at Adam's simple dress, "is at the back."

Adam ran over the menu while Gaspard waited, twirling the tips of his moustache. Then, no longer able to endure the suspenseful silence, the little man leaned forward.

"The seafood of the region," he made an emphatic pucker with his lips, "is superb!"

He spoke with an exotic French accent and murmured warmly as Adam chose one item after another from the menu.

"Ah yes," he glowed, "baked haddock with my own special stuffing and accompanied by rhubarb sauce. You cannot help but adore it."

But when Adam ordered wine Gaspard's eyebrows truly rose in respect. His eyes began to twinkle, and his face broke into a delighted smile.

"Ah, a most discerning choice. It is so rare to find someone familiar with fine wine. It will be a pleasure to serve you."

Celia was somewhat astonished as the little man trotted off. She turned to Adam.

"Well, you certainly hit it off. You an expert on fancy wine or something?"

Adam grinned, his eyes flecked with amber lights.

"Lucky guess, I suppose."

But the utter ease with which Adam lounged at the table seemed to say that here was a matter in which he did not make lucky guesses. He knew exactly what he was doing. Indeed, he seemed to fit into the surroundings. His smile seemed to add a glow to the room itself. His simple workingman's shirt sat on his shoulders with an elegance that is not bought – even for a fortune – but must come bred into the bone.

As evening darkened the room, Gaspard appeared. With a flourish, he lit the plump rosy candle on the table.

"There," he said, clasping his dimpled hands together enthusiastically, "it is so romantic! The wine, the food, they will be ready very soon."

When Gaspard appeared with a bottle, dewy in its chill, Adam swirled a portion of the pale liquid in his glass and nodded approvingly. Food followed, the heavenly aroma making

Celia realize she was ravenous. Gaspard fussed so charmingly, placing her plate just so, and Adam kept her wineglass full and laughed so merrily that soon enjoyment bubbled up from her heart. Once again, life was sweet. Time and this glorious golden man had worked their healing magic.

"You enjoyed yourself, didn't you?" Adam beamed when at last, stuffed, feted, and adrift in a wine-touched glow, the pair stepped out into the evening. "I like to see you laughing like that."

"How could I help it! Between the two of you I got waited on like some kind of princess. You aren't royalty out in disguise are you?"

Adam chuckled as he offered her his arm.

"Beats me! But if I am a lost prince I wish I'd remembered to bring a little more of my gold with me."

Gold! Grand and shining, the word swept through Celia's mind. Golden hair, golden eyes, golden face. You don't need any more gold, she thought. You don't!

And the memory came to her of how she had found him on the shore magnificently gilded by the morning sun. Her heart thumped so crazily she had to look away. Her eye fell on his hand where the dying light struck the big gold ring at his knuckle.

"Why . . . your ring," she cried impulsively.

"We never thought of it before. It might be some kind of clue. Oplin's Jewelry is open late. Let's drop in and see if he can help us."

Adam agreed genially, more to please her than from any desire to probe his own past.

"Sure. But I won't be responsible if it says, 'Made in Japan' on the inside."

Andy Oplin sometimes sold engagement rings to young couples. So when Adam and Celia walked in, he came to the counter with a hopeful smile.

"We are wondering if you could take a look at this ring," Adam twisted it from his finger, "and give us ... um, an appraisal."

Andy sighed. He hoped these people weren't going to try to sell him some dreadful piece of costume jewelry.

Adam and Celia watched silently while Andy switched on the bright light at his work table to examine the piece in minute detail. When he returned to the counter, his face wore a changed, somewhat awed expression.

"Solid gold, eighteen to twenty-two karat," he told them. "And the stones are top quality. A diamond and a natural ruby. I couldn't even think of buying a thing like that. Worth a fortune!"

The two young people looked at each other in startled bewilderment. Adam took the ring into the palm of his hand.

"Could you tell us anything else about it? Who made it, maybe, or where it came from?"

Andy shook his balding head.

"Nope. Workmanship's first class, of course. Likely American. And you'd be the only one to tell about the inscription inside it."

Inscription!

Adam and Celia both leaned over the ring, turning it in the light until the spidery lines came into view. Celia took one glance – and felt her heart turn over against her ribs.

"To my darling," it read. "Love, Lydia."

"Thanks." Adam's voice was strangely harsh. He shoved the ring into his pocket. The two of them hurried out into the night.

They headed straight for the truck, neither of them saying a word. Celia found herself struggling to regain the composure she had so suddenly and so wildly lost at the sight of the engraved line. And Adam seemed to have a tightly clamped jaw with the muscles around it worked up into knots. Only when he opened the truck door for Celia did he relax his shoulders and manage a little of his old nonchalant grin.

"Darned if I have the faintest idea who this Lydia could be."

Your sweetheart! Celia cried silently. Your fiancee! Or ... or your wife!

Outwardly, her answering smile was wan.

She started the truck and was glad that the driving took all her attention. The darkness made it impossible to read what was racing across her face. She ought to be happy, she told herself fiercely, that Adam had at least one clue to his past no matter how disturbing it turned out to be. After all, wasn't it quite foolish to suppose that a man as handsome and virile as he was should be without attachments. He could not float about in the never-never land of amnesia forever. The sooner everything came out into the open the better it would be for everybody – herself included.

Yet somehow she couldn't find the heart to make conversation. The hum of the engine and the bump of the tires on the deserted road seemed to fill the gap. The two of them stared hard into the blackness in front of them, each lost in a world the other could not penetrate.

It was only when they pulled up beside the darkened house and switched off the engine that the silence around them suddenly seemed as immense as the night itself. A giant moon hung so low over the sea that its gilded pathway shimmered almost to their very feet. In the distance, dark headlands loomed against a star-strewn indigo sky. And everywhere the soft air played with such a whisper of unbearable tenderness that Celia could not stop her heart from swelling in her breast.

For a moment, under the rustling maple, they stood enthralled. Then Adam's arms reached out, encircling the tremulous girl beside him, drawing her fiercely close.

"Celia," he murmured, his voice rough with emotion, "beautiful, dark-eyed Celia..."

His lips came down on hers with such warm sweetness that her starved soul all but cried out in ecstasy at being held again after so many, many lonely months.

For one moment, one long, enchanted moment, she lay within the circle of his embrace, letting the melting glory of his kiss wash through her quivering body, feeling doors she had thought shut up forever open at his touch.

Then the inscription from the ring burnt itself through her mind in letters of fire. She could not let herself go. Adam could not be hers. He belonged to someone called Lydia. In a few days, a few hours maybe, his memory would awaken. He would look at her and turn away as a sane man turns away from the meaningless ravings he has uttered aloud while in the grip of some delirium.

"Adam ... don't!"

With a pain like the tearing of her own flesh, she ripped herself out of his arms.

"We ... we can't. Lydia..."

The name fell from her lips like the cry of a

small bird wounded in the night. Turning, she fled up the steps to the lonely stronghold of her room before Adam had a chance to utter a whisper of protest.

CHAPTER THREE

The next morning Celia crept downstairs hoping that everyone else had finished eating. She had overslept, partly from exhaustion, partly from reluctance to face Adam across the breakfast table. Mercifully, the kitchen was deserted except for Aunt Meg. Celia made do with toast, which she washed down with the strong coffee left in the pot.

Aunt Meg, seeing the dark circle under the girl's eyes, stifled a sigh. Gavin had been gone for so long and Celia had seemed to finally brighten after Adam had arrived. The old woman supposed that Celia was again remembering that fateful drowning. She could not look into Celia's heart and see that Gavin had been replaced by a handsome stranger who also brought grief with him, like some kind of plague the girl could not escape.

Draining her cup, Celia stepped out into the morning sunshine. Though it was still early, the air was heating up. A heat haze shimmered just above the old rail fence. The tallest grasses were touched with yellow. From the maple a self-important cicada buzzed loudly among the leaves. Cicadas were so noisy yet so reclusive. In all her life Celia could not recall having actually seen one.

She hesitated, then made her way toward the barn where she found that all the customary chores were finished. The stable was clean and empty. The barnyard gate was open, indicating that the cattle had already been taken to the pasture. The black and white calves switched their tails contentedly, the telltale drops of breakfast still clinging to their whiskers.

Stillness reigned. The milking utensils gleamed from their scouring and sat neatly aligned on their shelves. The forks and shovels sat in a row. The concrete floor was so clean it seemed to have been washed. Adam had done all this, taking on the extra work so that she might have a little more rest in the morning. Somehow, it made her feel his tenderness again. Her throat caught.

"Adam," she whispered. "Oh Adam . . ."

She looked around again and another thought gripped her. Perhaps all this neatness masked a reproach. A reproach against running away from his kisses – against her cowardice in avoiding breakfast – against . . .

She straightened up. Look, she muttered to herself, stop being silly! It was only a kiss from a fellow you hardly know. In a few days he'll get his memory back and that will be that. It's nothing to get worked up about!

This little inner speech worked for a moment. After all, why get entangled with someone who might have a wife and five children. Taking a deep breath, she tried to chase the whole event out of her mind as if it were some annoying burr. But for one split second she could not help but think of laughing, fair-haired children and of that moment among the sage plants when she had longed so wistfully for a child of her own.

She turned, meaning to examine the blackberry bushes, when the drone of the tractor coming down the lane caught her. It was a load of hay. Uncle Bart was driving and Adam, like some fair prince of the hayfields, sat enthroned high atop the yellow bales. The two of them must have repaired the tractor and gone up to the fields without her help.

Another twinge hit her, thinking of the two men working up there without the extra driver that they needed. Oh well, she would just get herself out there to help with the next load.

When the wagon was pulled up to the elevator, Bart got down creakily from the tractor seat. Adam, with the surefooted ease of a big cat, slid along the side of the load and landed square on his feet in the summer dust. The back of his shirt was already stained damply from the work and the heat. Wisps of hay clung to the knees of his rapidly fading jeans.

Yet when he saw Celia coming, his eyes turned swiftly to the barn and the tan of his cheeks deepened visibly. Uncle Bart plugged in the elevator.

"You get this load started, girl. I'm taking Adam up to the mow to show him how to stack. I don't want half of it falling on my head when I go pulling out bales in the winter."

Adam seemed glad to go and Celia was just as glad not to be left alone on the wagon with him even though the clatter of the elevator made it just about impossible to say anything.

As soon as the two men disappeared into the barn she got out her bale hook and struggled until she had dislodged a few of the topmost bales and sent them up into the barn. That was the hardest part – making a hole in the tightly packed load for herself to work in.

She soon accomplished it. With footing and space she tugged the bales rapidly toward herself with her slim strong arms and hefted them by their twine onto the moving chain. In spite of their formidable size, the bales weren't nearly as heavy as they looked. With callouses in the right places and her slender body growing lithe and fit from the work, Celia found it wasn't really that hard at all. After all, had she not been helping out, either here or with her parents, ever since she had been big enough to reach the tractor clutch?

Now she threw herself into the work. She wished the wagonload were twice its size so that she would have to think of nothing but the strain on her muscles and the hot sun boring relentlessly into her back.

They managed to bring in another load before lunch. In the field, Celia managed to be looking at her knuckles when Adam wheeled past with the loader. Back at the barn, the rangy man went, very willingly, back up to the mow to help Bart.

At noon, Aunt Meg set out a great tureen of vegetable cream soup, thick brown, homemade bread, and strong tea. Adam ate with concentration while Celia spooned at her soup in barely hidden discomfort. Aunt Meg and Uncle Bart seemed tongue-tied. Silence hung around the table like a pall.

One more load that afternoon finished the field. Immediately, Bart hitched up the mower and set out to tackle the next hayfield. Adam, wanting to know how the mower worked, stuck to the old man's heels with the intentness of a large hunting dog.

Was he, Celia wondered, deliberately avoiding her?

She retired to the potato patch to attack the weeds with furious nervous energy. She felt filled with a restless inner storm, dreading the moment when she must face Adam.

Something indeed would have to be said. They couldn't go on dodging each other like a couple of awkward teenagers – not if they were going to work together – not if they had to endure the close daily rounds of the farm.

Much later, after dinner, it could not be told if she was the one who went out under the shady maple deliberately, or if it was he, or if it mattered. Celia only knew her throat went dry as his footsteps approached her softly from behind.

"Celia." The vibrant voice was close enough to make her jump. "I'm ... sorry about last night. I really had no right..."

"Oh," she shrugged, failing to be nonchalant. "There's nothing to worry about. It wasn't ... important."

Blood crept into her face as she said this and she couldn't look at him. There was a long moment of absolute silence. Then he had her by the shoulders, making her face him. The muscles of his jaw stood out in cords. His eyes blazed gold sparks at her.

"Wasn't it," he asked harshly. "Wasn't it at

all?"

She swallowed hard, saying nothing. Her eyes could not rise above his third shirt button. His fingers tightened momentarily, all but making her cry out in their grip. Then, letting go, his hands fell limply.

"I'm sorry," he said. "I seem to have this talent for doing the wrong thing. It was those ... great sad eyes of yours, like the color of spring earth touched with green. I wanted to fill them with laughter, but ... all I've managed to do is upset you. You're right to have none of me, when I don't know what I am or who I'm tied up with." He turned to her again. "A summer moon, a salt breeze can turn a fellow's head. It won't happen again."

"I ..."

"Not," his voice cut off, "at least, until my own life is straightened out."

With a shake of his bright head he was gone as swiftly as he had come, leaving Celia staring out at the sea, her heart jumping against her ribs.

"Not until!" The words sang in her heart like a promise. "Not until..."

Then she cut off the thought. Hope like that was too dangerous. A gorgeous man such as Adam could not help but have been snapped up years before. If once she let herself want him, if once she let her foolish heart...

64

It was enough to remember the tearing agony when that fisherman had told her about Gavin's boat. No, she couldn't stand it. Not a second time. Better her heart should freeze. Better no man at all than that dreadful pain all over again!

By the time she went to bed, her mind had become a carefully composed blank. She had opened the window to let in the sea air, planning a calm night's sleep in its coolness. But when she finally closed her eyes, she tossed and shifted, her curls tangled in the moonlight.

But it wasn't Gavin's name she whispered, but that of the golden stranger creeping irrevocably into her heart.

With the first light of dawn she got up, slipped a certain small and cherished diamond from her hand, and laid it to rest forever in its satin-lined box in her drawer.

At breakfast, everyone was subdued. Adam forked down eggs and bacon while Celia settled for a cup of scalding coffee to brace her for the day. She fed the calves, drove the cows to their pasture, and went to check for potato bugs. Adam rode off on the back of the tractor. A short while later the metallic whirr of the mower drifted down from the high field. The bottom of the mow was barely covered. Hundreds and hundreds more bales would be needed to see the dairy herd through the winter.

Adam was following the course of the machine and would soon, no doubt, be driving it. Cutting hay was touchy business. The hay itself, in order to be nutritious, could be neither too green nor too tough. The corners had to be squared to prevent wastage. Stones had to be avoided and care taken around all animals or people, for the deadly blade could take off a hand or a foot in a second.

The heat increased, becoming dampish and sticky. The sun retreated into a white haze. An erratic breeze suddenly blew up an edge of ragged rainclouds against the restless sky. Soon the tractor, with the mower rattling behind, was speeding down the lane and making for the machine shed. It got inside in time, but the downpour started before the two men managed to reach the shelter of the house.

Bart was rain-spattered and disgruntled. Adam, his hair dampened into streaks, looked happily invigorated. He grinned through white teeth as they made their way into the kitchen.

"We got caught," he laughed. "Came right down before we could even get under a tree."

A bar of wetness lay across his broad shoulders and his jeans were damp, yet he shifted in them comfortably, as if the coolness on his skin felt good.

"Huh," Bart was grouching, "I won't be

able to cut again today. Not till this lot's dried up. Stuff already down might just rot if the wet keeps up."

A pot of tea and some crumbly oatmeal cookies cheered him up, and the rain proved vehement but brief. Soon Bart was eyeing the tears in the clouds that were already scudding toward the horizon.

"Well, plenty to do close to home – couple of mower blades to sharpen and I should get down that new drum of diesel oil. Rake could stand a few new teeth, too. Stones play the devil with it."

Adam looked up.

"Maybe you could show me..."

"Sure, sure. You weren't half bad on the mower this morning. I'll teach you how to change blades. They're touchy things. Break to bits if they're not just right."

The pair stamped out, leaving prints in the dampened dust. They went into the end of the machine shed which was fixed up with tools as a bit of a shop. Celia knew that in a few moments Adam would be put to slaving with a whetstone over the dozens of little triangular teeth. Adam had, as yet, no suspicion of the monotony of this task.

She herself soon followed, taking a deep, deep breath of the rain-sweetened air. The sun flickered through a rift in the cloud and in a

67

moment transformed the dripping leaves and grass into diamond sparkles. A spider's web strung inside the lilac bush became an intricate filigree of miniature gems. The maple turned into layers upon layers of polished, shimmering green.

Usually, at times like these, Uncle Bart would end up calling Celia over to hold something for him while he hammered, or to reach with her slender fingers into some crevice of machinery which would not admit his own gnarled paws.

But today he had Adam. Celia felt faintly left out. Oh well, she ought to dust the potato plants against bugs now that the wind had died and the wet leaves would hold the powder. On her way to find her gardening gloves she caught sight through the dusty glass of two figures moving about. Masculine laughter broke out periodically. How well, she thought, the two of them seemed to be getting along.

With a sigh, Celia set to work, the rich soil clinging in little damp clumps to the edges of her shoes. She found a few of the orange larvae and sprinkled the powder somewhat heavily as a precautionary measure. There were quite a number of weeds pushing up in the center of the rows. With the moisture from the rain they would really jump. She just ought to have a run up and down the middles with the rototiller while she had the chance.

The machine was kept in a little shed at the far corner of the garden and, like every other piece of equipment around the place, it was old and heavy. Propping the door wide, she tugged with all her might to get it over the threshold. One wheel sank into the decaying floor and Celia wrenched in vain. Then a strong hand slid past her to take hold of the handles.

"Here," Adam said. "Let me. This is quite a big outfit."

His sudden nearness made her throat close in shock. His arm brushed her shoulder – with the effect of electric sparks. She had to press herself against his hard broad chest in order to clear the doorway for him.

"Th ... thank you. It is rather ... hard to get that thing out through the door."

"Why didn't you call me? I was just going around with your Uncle Bart to..."

From behind the machine shed, a crash and a shout froze their words. Then, like a pair of startled racehorses, they went galloping around to see what was the matter.

When they did see, Celia let out a scream of alarm. The high platform on which Bart stored his great drums of diesel oil had collapsed at one corner and the other threatened to go in a moment. Her uncle was caught straining against this frame, unable either to hold it up or to escape the fully filled steel drum which hovered above his head, about to roll down and crush the old man with its deadly weight.

In a flash, Adam had his shoulder under the platform.

"Get him away," he yelled to Celia, "get him out of the way."

Celia grabbed her uncle by the elbow and pulled him back with such frightened force that the two of them ended up in a heap a couple of yards away – still in the direct path of the tottering drum.

Adam took in the situation with a vivid golden glance. Then, with a cat-like speed too swift for the eye to follow, he let go of the platform and, even as it crashed, took the full weight of the oil barrel with the flat of his chest. Then, before it could flatten him backwards, he twisted his body with agility, deflecting the force sideways. Grasping both ends of the oil barrel as it fell, he slowed its precipitous descent to the ground and ended by bringing the massive thing to a halt in the corner.

Both Celia and Bart stared at him in amazement.

"Holy mackeral, lad, but you're quick on your feet. Usually takes two men to lift that thing."

"Well," murmured Adam, "couldn't let it

fall on you, sir. Or on ... Celia."

His look, brief as it was, made her stomach tremble. Their eyes locked for a fraction of a second, then Adam looked briskly away. By the time he was helping her up, he had become completely impersonal.

And yet ... she had the wildest impression that his hand, as it gripped her, was shaking.

Uncle Bart made a brief effort to rise, then subsided with a groan. The two younger people turned in alarm.

"Uncle Bart, what is it? Are you all right?"

"Oh ... I guess I've put my back out. Can't move. Did this once before when you were off in the city. Go get your Aunt Meg."

Like a young deer, Celia sped toward the house, wondering all the while why she had not heard one word about her uncle's back in all the letters they had written. That was just like them, keeping their problems from her so she could enjoy herself without any worry.

Aunt Meg came flying, her face knit up in worry, her arms full of pillows and sofa cushions.

"Last time he was laid up three weeks," she told her niece. "I hope this time it isn't any worse!"

When she got to Uncle Bart, she surveyed him anxiously.

"I called the doctor. He says you're not to

move until he gets here. Heaven knows what you've thrown out of joint this time!"

She was torn between affectionate scolding and a worry she could barely hide. Back and forth she paced, working herself up more and more until Adam took her by the shoulders. His grip was gentle but would not brook resistance as he led her to an upturned crate.

"Just sit down, Mrs. Walton. Take it easy until the doctor comes."

Aunt Meg sat down meekly, for Adam, by his very presence, seemed to radiate calm. With unconscious ease he put himself in charge of the situation. He stood in the sun like some magnificent pillar anyone could lean on.

And so they remained until Dr. Morgan bustled up with his bag.

"Well well, Bart, what have you done to yourself now? Seems I make this place a regular stop."

Bart grinned feebly.

"My back. Just like the last time. And I'm lucky that's all. If it hadn't been for Adam here, I'd have been squashed flat under that drum of diesel oil over there."

Dr. Morgan was treated to the story, after which he cast an appraising glance at the blond, muscular man.

"Well then, he's good luck for you, Bart. Washed right up onto your doorstep."

Bart nodded vigorously.

"Yep, sure got to agree with you there!"

In spite of his pain, the old fellow cast a look at Celia which Adam, mercifully, didn't see. The girl scuffed the earth with her toe hoping no one noticed her burning ears.

The doctor turned his attention to the farmer's back, exploring very carefully with his fingers. Then he paused, gathered himself, and made a sudden and decisive thrust with the heels of his hands.

"Yeeoww!" Bart yelped. "You tryin' to punch a hole clear through me?"

"Slipped disc, Bart. Just putting it back where it belongs."

"Well then ... oooh ... oowww, that the ... ouch ..."

The doctor put an end to Bart's efforts to rise with a quick grasp.

"I said not to move. Slipped disc is only part of the story. You better get used to the idea of spending time flat on your back while this lot gets better."

"Stay in bed! This time of year! I ... ooowww."

Dr. Morgan peered at the farmer over his spectacles, this time not trying to restrain him. It only took one good twist to make Bart keep still of his own accord.

"I'm telling you, Bart, if you don't stop

wriggling you're going to be sorry. It's going to be hard enough getting you up to the house and into your bed."

Several plans were suggested, from fashioning a stretcher to ferrying Bart in the back of the pickup truck. But each time Dr. Morgan and Adam tried to move him, Bart let out such a groan that they had to set him back on his pillows. The doctor tugged at his chin in perplexity.

"This one's a poser. I don't see how we can get him along without any jars."

Adam looked down at the old man who had befriended him, now sprawled painfully on the ground.

"If I carried him myself, do you think..."

"You couldn't. Not all the way to the house."

"If I have to," Adam said quietly, "I can. Just let me try."

Bending down, he slid his arms under the wounded man with infinite care. Then, as if he were lifting a hundred and sixty pounds of nitroglycerine, he began to raise the weight into the air. Uncle Bart groaned. Adam froze. Then the old man sputtered impatiently.

"For heavens sake, keep going lad. It's not nearly as bad as when the two of you tried swinging me around together."

Shifting his arms ever so lightly, seeking

74

some hidden point of balance, Adam got to his feet. Cords stood out along his neck, muscles bulged against the fabric of his shirt, but he kept moving. Slowly, steadily, step by smooth gliding step he walked until he reached the door of the house. Celia rushed ahead to open it.

Once inside, there was the obstacle of the staircase. Adam, showing sign of neither weakness or hesitation, proceeded to mount the steps one by one, keeping his burden perfectly centered. A few moments later, Bart was carefully deposited between the covers which Meg had pulled back.

"There," Adam grinned, "In bed like a gentleman. Nothing to do now but take it easy."

Bart uttered a crusty grunt but he could not conceal the fact that the mattress was heaven to him. The doctor came in behind, puffing slightly from the stairs.

"All right, Bart, the ticket now is for you to lie still and get waited on hand and foot. In about a month or so, you'll be up and strolling around. Lot longer, though, before you go lifting anything heavy."

"A month!" Bart croaked. "In the middle of haying season! And what about the milking and the . . ."

"Don't worry, sir," Adam cut in, casting a

glance at the girl beside him. "We can take care of that, Celia and I."

Why was it that one look from him was enough to make Celia's heart quiver in her breast?

"But you've scarcely been here a week or two!"

"I know, I know. And I'll probably make mistakes – that is, if Celia doesn't keep an eye on me. But I'll certainly do my best."

Bart subsided, gratitude and skepticism mixed in his glance. Yet the manicured hands were already roughened by work and the fellow was getting a decent tan. Maybe, just maybe, he might come through on his promise.

"Well," Bart sighed, worn out from the accident, "we'll see."

They left Meg fussing with the sheets and followed the doctor downstairs. He harrumphed loudly as he made for his car.

"It's not as bad as it looks," he told them. "Just severe back strain. But he's got to lie still until I say he can get up. The old coot is stubborn as a wooden mule!"

"Oh, he'll stay in bed," said Celia firmly. "Aunt Meg and I will see to that!"

"You do that girl. And don't go telling him about any foul ups on the farm unless you absolutely have to. He'll be trying to get up and straighten things."

"Nothing's going to foul up," Adam said. "If I can possibly help it!"

The deep quiet voice somehow made the idea of trouble seem ridiculous and Celia couldn't help glancing at him. He stood with his feet planted wide apart and his strong arms folded across his chest. Confidence flowed from him in such an invincible tide that anyone would have thought he had been born on the farm. Suddenly, the alarm that had gripped Celia since she had first seen her uncle hurt evaporated and, for the first time, she was able to relax.

But ever so slightly, she shook her head.

I mustn't trust him like this, she told herself. He really ... doesn't know what he's promising!

But she was glad he had promised. Once again, she had the sense of a rock beneath her feet.

The sun was slanting alarmingly low as the doctor bumped off down the lane. The last remnants of cloud drifted toward the horizon like the banners of a retreating army. Celia reflected that in an emergency, hours can flash by like minutes.

For a moment she allowed herself to gaze at the vast sea now flecked with aquamarine and topaz. Droplets of rain still glistened on blue devil flowers and pricked out specks of silver on

77

the chicory. When Adam came quietly on her side, she did not move. She listened to the strong slow evenness of his breathing. She could almost imagine the red blood coursing through his veins, the warmth of his tanned skin touching hers...

There she was again, falling into the trap. She tore her eyes away from the lovely scene.

"I better go get the cows. It'll take us a while to finish the milking."

Taking her customary shortcut along the shore, she padded across rain-dampened sand. Long waves flung fingers of foam at her feet but she did not step back, for the menace seemed gone from the water now, along with her anger. She was ready to declare a truce with the sea. For after all, had it not brought to her a lithe, golden man? Perhaps...

But there were too many "perhaps"'s in her life. Best just to take the peace that came from Adam like a gift and ask no questions.

The cows were bunched against the gate, gazing reproachfully at Celia for being so late. Their hides were glossier for the wetting as they jostled impatiently into the lane and their hooves made great splayed prints on the earth.

When they reached the stable, they found the door open in readiness and a waiting treat of dairy ration in each of their places. They munched greedily, accepting Adam without a quiver as he walked among them, clicking shut the neckpieces and giving each an affectionate rub. The milkers sat gleaming on the cement floor, ready to be attached. The pail of warm water and disinfectant waited for Celia to take the sponge and wash the udder of each cow.

Celia marveled at how effortlessly the two of them fell into an easy pattern. Without Uncle Bart to supervise she had expected some awkwardness, but they both knew the routine by rote. Now they were working together as if they had been doing it for years. Soon pails of foaming milk were being poured into the cooling tank and the bellows of the calves were silenced by a hearty dinner. Even Milly, the independent orange barn cat, deigned to make one of her appearances, lapping daintily from a pan provided for her use.

The difference was the silence, as if Celia and Adam were afraid to speak to each other. Absorbed in the tasks at hand and aware of the lateness of the hour, they passed close and helped each other, yet all the while they managed to avoid looking in each other's eyes.

And yet ... already there was a powerful rhythm between them. They complimented each other. When Adam released a cow, it was Celia who shooed it into the barnyard. Celia mixed hot water and powerful cleanser. Adam took the stiff brush and scrubbed milking utensils until they shone. Then Celia placed each item on its shelf as he was finished. Celia swept the concrete. Adam, with the grin he always had when he did this job, took up the shovel and cleaned out the gutters.

Only when the last task was finished and the cows drowsed in the little side enclosure where they spent the night, did Adam speak.

"Well," he said, "that's one good job done. Do you think we can manage the rest, you and I?"

This time she found the courage to meet his disturbing golden eyes. A tiny wellspring of assurance bubbled up. She smiled the tiniest half smile.

"Yes ... yes, I think we can. The ... two of us!"

Instantly his brilliant smile burst out, lighting not only his own face but hers as well, like some afterflash of the slowly sinking sun.

Then he lifted his hand, and there was no answering flash.

For the first time that day, Celia noticed that the heavy, glittering ring was gone.

The following morning, Celia found herself springing out of bed with the first light of the dawn. She seemed charged with an energy whose source she did not examine. She only knew that the cows had to be milked and the cooler filled before the big tank pulled in to pick up the milk.

And then there was that hay. It had to be somehow raked and baled and gotten into the barn.

The milking went even more smoothly than it had the evening before and they looked in on Uncle Bart just after breakfast. The pain had already receded from his face, to be replaced by disgruntlement. He squinted out the window at the brilliant sun already plowing its way through a cloudless sky.

"Drat this back! Would have been a great day to get some more of that hay cut."

"Well," put in Adam, "if it's a good day for cutting hay, then the hay will be cut."

"But..."

"I know, but I've seen how the mower works. I'm sure I can run it now."

"Maybe you better hold off. In a few days when I'm up and around, I'll..."

"Few days!" Meg snorted. "You know better than to try. Doctor would conk you over the head with his bag!"

"Oh that doctor! Full of prunes. Look here, I ... yeeeouch!"

"See," said Meg in a softer voice as her husband sank back upon his pillow. "Now you take it easy."

Celia walked over to her uncle's side.

"You know the hay would be dried to a crisp

if we wait. I'm sure Adam can handle the machinery perfectly."

Bart knotted his brows. Then he gave out a long sigh and a resigned, crooked smile.

"Well, just don't either of you go cutting off your fool feet in that thing. It's damned dangerous if you don't know what you're doing."

As Celia followed Adam out into the hall, she looked at his tall form walking ahead of her. Her heart was full of confidence but her head was full of doubt. Lord, if there was another accident . . .

Prudently, she kept her doubt to herself and put her trust in the broad easy set of his shoulders. Really, she reasoned, under the circumstances what else could she do?

He held the gate open as she drove the cattle out toward the pasture and gave her an easy smile. She smiled back, then hurried on, hoping he wouldn't see the flush rising on her cheeks. If she were going to work with the man, she told herself, she would certainly have to stop the blushing. She would have to become impervious to his charms – pretend he was simply an acquaintance. Someone she had to co-operate with. Someone . . .

Someone who could reach out at any time and put his hand around her waiting heart!

She allowed herself a rueful smile. So much

for resolutions.

As she swung back along the shore, the brightness dancing on the waves must have had an effect. In spite of the trouble at the house, in spite of the wrenching scene with Adam that evening after the restaurant, she felt her spirits lifting up and up. After all, maybe that ring was a family heirloom and Lydia was Adam's great great grandmother. Or maybe it was estate jewelry, or a relic, or a gift from some particularly gushy friend.

Oh maybe, maybe. There were a thousand possibilities.

And if Celia were a smart girl, she wouldn't let herself think about a single one of them!

She reached the barn only in time to see Adam driving the tractor up the lane toward the partly cut meadow. As she saw him turn into the field and get down to adjust the mower, Celia swallowed quickly. Then, scarcely realizing what she was doing, she began to hike after him with all the speed she could muster. He really had very little experience operating that thing, and if he wasn't careful...

By the time she made it up the long grade to the gate of the field her heart was pumping overtime and she panted hotly. Adam had already thrown the tractor into gear, engaged the power takeoff, and was about to lift his foot from the clutch.

Unreasoning alarm filled Celia. She leaped forward.

"Adam, oh Adam, look out. You don't know . . ."

Her voice trailed off, drowned suddenly in a crisp clatter of machinery. The tractor moved forward, the cutting bar bobbed, the long whirring blade bit into a swathe of summer sweet hay. Timothy, clover, yellow-eyed daisies shivered and fell in regiments. The mower ran smoothly, the tractor purred. Nothing jammed, screeched, or flew apart.

The trembling girl let out a long breath and felt like an idiot. She retreated behind a stand of prickly ash where she would not be seen. She watched Adam riding high in the seat, keeping the wheel parallel with the uncut hay, while keeping watch on the mower with swift backward glances. At the corner, he made a skillful maneuver which preserved the carefully defined square of hay. If he was no farmer, Celia thought, he was certainly used to driving.

But driving what?

Something low, perhaps, and powerful, with an open top and a way of ripping past other drivers as if they were standing still.

Retreating down the corridor of the lane, she made her way back to the barn. Adam was doing fine and her fears were foolish. She had best see what she could do about the weeds in her garden. As soon as the baling started she wouldn't have a minute for her little plants.

The scent of new-mown hay, a perfume like no other in the world, seemed to follow her. She breathed it with closed eyes, thinking that it was at moments like these that she loved the country with all her heart. Then she roused herself, bustling off to the many tasks that cried out to be done.

The rain had sprouted weeds by the thousands so that they spread underfoot like a low thick carpet. Most were scarcely an inch high and not thicker than a sewing thread. But once allowed to put down a root and leap upward, they would quickly reach a size where it took both her hands to pull them out. It was better to get them now while they were young.

She cleared the centers of the rows with the rototiller, then attacked the ones between the carrots with her hoe. But often she paused to rest and let her eyes stray quietly to the tall figure riding back and forth high up in the fields. Each time he turned the sun caught his hair, sending back a glint of gold across the lush summer green of the land.

The hay, including the bit Bart had cut, dried that afternoon and in the morning was ready to be raked. While the windrows cured further in the hot sun, Adam addressed himself to the problem of attaching the cantankerous baler to the tractor and threading it with fresh twine.

Again his easy touched showed itself. Where even Bart used to struggle and swear each time he had to hook up the driveshaft, Adam's hands made the tricky fittings slide together in a single thrust.

When it came to the twine, he rocked on his heels for a moment, frowning at the complicated path. Yet no sooner had Celia appeared to see if she could help, when he gave a small private nod of satisfaction that said, "Now I remember", and he ran the twine unerringly through all the complex loops and holes.

Why, thought Celia, he really does have a kind of magic in his hands.

Celia inspected his handiwork and could find no fault. The tension was just right – the little knives raised to snip the twine as soon as each knot was tied.

Baling began after a great handful of hay had been taken to Uncle Bart so that he could feel its condition with his horny old hands.

"Got it cut, did you?" he asked, managing to sound both pleased and astonished. "Well, feels just about right to me. Bale her too dry and the cows won't eat it. Bale her too wet and you get bales like boulders – liable to heat up in

86

the barn, too. Spontaneous combustion. Burn the whole outfit to the ground!"

Adam folded his arms.

"Well, Mr. Walton, Celia and I will get on the job right away."

They set out for the field and, with excitement flickering through her, Celia edged the baler up to the first windrow which was as neatly raked as anything her uncle could do. Throwing the engine into gear, she felt the driveshaft engage and saw the teeth of the pickup begin to turn and lift the hay into the maw of the baler. Behind it, Adam rode the stacker, balancing on his feet with the unerring grace of an athlete as he built and dropped pyramid after pyramid of bales behind him. Each time Celia looked he flashed his smile while he worked tirelessly on and on until it came time to break for lunch.

The old baler, whether through some whim or through Adam's skill, ran smoothly all afternoon. Celia drove while the man behind worked in the blazing sun. Every hour they made a trip to the shade of the butternut tree where a jug sat waiting to slake their thirst. Though Aunt Meg had offered to make lemonade, iced tea, orange juice, or anything they fancied, Adam insisted on spring water.

"Delicious," he grinned. "Wouldn't drink anything else out there in the sun."

The last time they had pulled over, he wiped his brow and handed the jug to Celia.

"Ladies first. Drink up!"

Since they had forgotten to bring a cup, Celia had to drink from one side of the jug, drawing in the cool sweetness to soothe her sticky throat.

Adam himself threw back his head, letting the clear water splash from the corners of his mouth and onto the broad planes of his chest. His eyes were closed in delight, his face thrown into strong relief against the afternoon sun which burnished his hair and made his lashes seem dusted with gold. Celia, unable to take her eyes from the rippling muscles of his throat as he swallowed, was reminded again of the sea god she supposed she had stumbled upon on the shore. Only now, energy seemed to crackle about him in invisible sparks as the work made him stronger and stronger.

Adam stopped drinking so abruptly that he caught her staring at him. A jaunty grin started across his lips, then stopped, as if overwhelmed. Slowly he put down the jug. He took a step, a single step toward her, before he stopped himself, his eyes glowing in their depths with tiny crisps of golden fire.

For a second his look held hers. Then, just as swiftly, he turned away.

"We ... better get going," he said. "We

should finish this field by supper time."

Despite the water, Celia's mouth had gone strangely dry. She leaped onto the tractor seat and thrust the throttle to a roar – to drown out the rushing in her own ears.

By chore time the moment had vanished. In the stable, Adam was his easy grinning self again, weaving a net of small courtesies about Celia. The sense of someone near her, quietly caring, was heady, intoxicating. The scent of fresh milk and new-stored hay permeated the air and the girl moved like a dreamer inside a contentment which was settling around her like a warm mist.

CHAPTER FOUR

The next morning, Adam was charged with even more energy than before. They ought to have gotten out the hay wagon and brought in the bales that were already waiting, but the wide sky, clear and polished as a blue mirror, made Adam look at the fields yet uncut.

"The heat will dry out the standing hay," he said. "Why don't we just cut another field or two and bale them up now? That way the hay is better and we can bring the lot at once."

"Well . . . Uncle Bart always does one field at a time, in case of rain."

"Oh it isn't going to rain. Just look at that sky. It'll be dry for days and days. Make hay while the sun shines, isn't that what farmers say?"

Celia hesitated, torn between fear of rain and the knowledge that the uncut hay was, indeed, drying up. Finally, swept along by Adam's enthusiasm, she went along. In the following days they had cut and baled two more fields before thinking about hauling the crop into the barn.

Uncle Bart wasn't pleased when he heard.

"Come a good downpour and the bales'll be soaked through. Ruin the lot!"

Adam raised his eyebrows.

"It hasn't shown any sign of rain yet. I'm sure we can get it all in in time."

Through most of one day, Adam and Celia worked at bringing in the bales, but it seemed they hardly made a dent in the number to be drawn in. A second day's work under the blue ceramic sky brought them close to the halfway mark. But on the third day, their luck seemed to have run out.

The morning dawned furnace hot – but not the dry heat of the previous days. This time it was the muggy sticky intolerable heat that clogs the slightest breeze and forebodes rain. As yet

90

there were no clouds, but the sky had thickened into a dull white through which the sun was but a molten blur sizzling the air below.

Aunt Meg stood at the kitchen door drying her hands on a tea towel.

"Storm for sure," she predicted. "Big one. Just look at that horizon."

The sea and the sky would have melded into one syrupy heat haze had it not been for a distant purple line running across the edge of the sky like a smear.

Three sets of eyes went to the many bales that still dotted the slopes. It was vital that this, the choicest part of the hay crop, escape. For the first time, doubt and dismay entered Adam's face.

"I thought... I was so sure we could get them in. Maybe I should have listened to you, Celia. If it really pours we could lose an awful lot."

Celia, well aware of the danger, rallied to his side.

"We can get it in, Adam, if we really get moving on the job. I don't think the rain will come until near evening."

The thought was like a challenge, prickling with its own excitement. Their eyes met. Suddenly they grinned at each other.

"All right," Adam cried. "You've got a deal.

Let's go!"

Off they rattled up the lane to load the first wagon of the day. Their spirits rose. They were as one as they threw themselves into the common task ahead. Indeed, despite the murderous heat they worked faster and better than they ever had before. Celia seemed to run the loader with unerring skill, never upsetting a single pile of bales across the ground. Adam, on the wagon, pulled the hay away as swiftly as he could set it down and soon the wagon was stacked into a mighty load at least two tiers higher than even Uncle Bart had dared to build it.

Celia, of course, now had to do all the unloading by herself, but at least she was out in the open where any chance movement of the air might cool her a little. Adam took on the stacking inside the barn where the still air, trapped under the sheet metal roof, was heated up to an incredible temperature.

After each load he would emerge, caked with pale rime and dripping with perspiration. Yet he would just give himself a splash at the stable tap and leap grinning onto the wagon ready for another trip. And Celia, grinning back, would drive off, for as long as Adam was with her nothing could diminish her energy.

They worked unflaggingly until noon, when the heat haze thickened to the point of being almost palpable and the sun was but a white smudge high overhead. In the house they barely paused to eat, only putting away a couple of sandwiches and about a gallon of iced tea. Aunt Meg hustled after them as they scrambled away from the table.

"You two just take it easier," she called in vain. "You're going to give yourselves heat stroke!"

Adam and Celia exchanged a silent glance and Adam paused.

"Listen Celia, we've been going like gangbusters. You're not..."

"No," cried Celia, "I'm not tired. I can go on all day."

"With you," she added silently, and climbed up again to her tractor seat even though the metal of the machine had become almost too hot to touch. Behind her the purple line on the horizon had fattened into an ominous ridge, warning them to speed all the faster.

Though the air had become like thick molasses and the heat was drawn into their lungs with every breath, the rest of the afternoon was almost like a ballet – a dance of intimate co-operation between interlocking machines, hard young bodies working joyfully, kindred spirits able to anticipate each other's every move without even the prompting of a word or a look.

As the cloud ridge began to grow into livid towers the two began to race in earnest, back and forth between barn and field.

"How are you doing?" Adam called. "Still holding up OK?"

"You kidding?" she shouted back over the snort of the motor. "Why I could go on like this for weeks!"

"Great! That's my girl! You've got spunk."

"My girl!" Celia tried to pretend she hadn't heard those words – but inside, she was floating.

As the afternoon dragged on she worked like a slim, curly-headed fury. Her yellow blouse stuck to her in patches, her jeans were coming out in holes where she used her knee to hoist the bales, her gloves were so worn through by twine that her skin was chaffed and bleeding in places. She sweltered inside the thick socks, stout shoes and long pants she had to wear to protect herself from the hay, and her muscles began to protest with every move.

But she wasn't tired! What was happening to her, she wondered. Why did she feel able to go on working forever as long as Adam was by her side?

She didn't have to answer. In her heart she knew.

She knew it was love!

The burgeoning storm had grown until it was

94

almost over their heads, but the bales out in the field had dwindled until there was just one more load to go. As they bumped back up the lane and through the gate, thunder rolled and lightning, like the yellow tongues of serpents, flicked from cloud to cloud. This threat only fueled the exhilaration of the two young people below.

"Come on," Celia whooped, "we can do it! Let's go!"

After all their work they could not – would not – let these last few bales get wetted by the rain.

Celia sped out the stubble on the loader, scooping up stook after stook. Adam, who had long since discarded his dusty shirt, stood high atop the load like some magnificent bronze-gold lord of the open fields, claiming his bales of tribute from the earth.

And each time Celia saw the ripple of his powerful muscles, caught the flash of his smile, her heart quickened, and she adored all the more her glorious golden man from the sea.

The still air had been swept into turmoil by the first of the storm winds as the wagon pulled up to the elevator. The sky overhead was blackened with a roil of cloud pouring inkily towards the opposite horizon. Celia breathlessly tugged bale after bale onto the elevator. High above, she caught glimpses of Adam working under the cramped peak of the roof. There was barely room left in the overflowing mow for this last load. As she finally tossed the last bale onto the elevator, lightning struck somewhere not far down the shore and a tremendous crash of thunder made her jump.

She watched for Adam, however, and would not budge from the wagon. Soon she saw him emerge from the small door under the eaves, and hop onto the spidery frame of the elevator, completely disregarding the way it swayed and quivered under his weight. In a few seconds he landed on his feet beside her with catlike agility.

Startled, Celia turned so quickly that she stumbled. Immediately, two strong hands had her by the shoulders, steadying her. The girl tried to make some joking comment – then saw the way he was looking at her.

Her lips parted, and her heart began to thud against her ribs. She seemed utterly, helplessly held, not by the hands, but by those fiercely glowing, gold-flecked eyes. Suddenly she felt weak in his grip, scarcely able to draw breath into her lungs. He leaned toward her, his voice was husky with desire.

"Celia," he murmured, "we cannot work together like this and pretend nothing is happening. I'm ... no closer to remembering my past. I don't care if I ever do. I've found ...

happiness here. All that matters to me now is the future. The future ... and you ..."

His voice trailed away and his fingers tightened. Celia felt his eyes drawing her towards an irresistible whirlpool into which she was willing to plunge forever. If he didn't care who he was, she didn't either. She would take his hand and stride boldly into that unknown future. She would, if she could, shout her love into the wild storm winds whistling up around them.

Her throat went tight, her hand rose slowly up to brush his cheek.

"Adam," she whispered, "Oh ... Adam ..."

Lightning seared above their heads in veins of living fire and the first great drops of the downpour splashed their backs, but neither noticed. Adam's bare bronzed arms slid around the girl's slim shoulders. He drew her to him until she lay pressed against the hard breadth of his chest. Her head tilted back. She felt the first light brush of the kiss that would bind them forever.

The rude crunch of tires and the violent slam of a car door shattered the spell. Startled as a bird, Celia jerked away. Adam swung angrily to see who had dared disturb them.

Then they both stared!

What met their astonished eyes was a large silver-grey Mercedes which had practically forced its aristocratic snout into the gate of the barnyard. Wildly incongruous, it gleamed in the stormy light like an ingot of silver tossed onto a homespun cloak.

But the woman who stepped out of it was even more startling. She was tall, model-thin, and devastatingly elegant. Her green muted suit declared in every tailored line that it had cost the earth. Her blue-black hair swept into a shining cap not even the blustering wind could ruffle. Her face, with its pale skin, marvelously high cheekbones and perfectly sculpted chin, would have been extremely beautiful had it not been twisted into a grimace of outraged shock.

She stood frozen. Then, by some operation of the will, she turned her look into one of delighted surprise. She then propelled herself forward, even running a few steps, though she was careful where she put her feet.

"Oh Peter," she cried. "Peter, I've found you! Oh we were all so sure you were drowned!"

Her heel sank into a hole so that her arms, which had been raised as if for an embrace, had to flail outward to help her catch her balance. Walking more slowly, she made her way up to where the two stood speechless.

"Peter, for heavens sake! Don't just stand there! I've driven all the way from Boston!"

She held up a fine slim clutch bag in an effort

to fend off the few random raindrops. Adam blinked.

"I'm afraid I . . ."

"Oh yes, I forgot." The bag made a small, irritated movement. "The police told me some incredible tale about amnesia or something. I'm Lydia, Peter. Lydia Burke. Your fiancee. You were sailing to Boston to be married!"

If this woman had set off a stick of dynamite at their feet, she could not have had a greater effect. A strangled sound of amazement issued from Adam's throat. Celia's hands flew up to her mouth. She gasped. Each word had struck like a stone aimed to kill.

Then a kind of blinding shock set in so that the girl could not even see her own fingers, let alone the sudden narrowing of Lydia's green eyes and the long mouth that relaxed and turning slightly up at the corners as she perceived her message hitting home.

Adam, in the meantime, stood staring at Lydia as if she were a two-headed wonder dropped from the sky. He might have remained there, petrified, had not the random spots condensed themselves into a sudden spurt. He started to say something but his voice was lost in a tremendous crash of thunder and a hiss of lightning blazing into a tree just on the edge of the hayfield. Celia shuddered and Lydia screamed outright.

"Oh – my suit! My shoes!"

Jolted alive, Adam swept Celia off the wagon with both his arms and set her swiftly on the ground. Then, taking each of them by the arm, he began to run in long quick strides until he managed to shove them both through the kitchen door just as the clouds broke, spewing sheets of water that filled the hollows in seconds and pounded on the roof like a thousand hammers.

Lydia, though she had escaped with only a couple of wet spots on her shoulders, shivered within her clothes as if they were soaking wet. Removing one of her shoes, she rubbed her instep which had supposedly suffered over the rough ground.

"Goodness, Peter," she muttered, "you could run a girl off her feet!"

She straightened, regaining her dignity when she noticed Aunt Meg standing with the teapot in one hand, her mouth open in amazement at this fashionable apparition which had blown into her kitchen. Since both Celia and Adam seemed tongue-tied, the Boston woman took it upon herself to inform Meg that she was Peter's fiancee and that she had come to collect him after his "terrible ordeal at sea".

Meg appeared to have as much difficulty grasping the situation as the other people in the room. Lydia stood looking about waiting for someone to say something. When no one moved, she turned to Adam, laying her hand on his arm in a small intimate gesture and beginning to smile.

"Peter, darling, this *has* been a shock for you, hasn't it? You do remember me, surely!"

Adam's brow knitted.

"I'm afraid I don't quite..."

"Peter, I'm Lydia Burke. The Boston Burkes! We've been engaged for simply ages. You can't imagine the furore when your yacht disappeared. Mama was frantic, what with the caterers and the florists and the wedding only two days away. Everyone said you should have never sailed out by yourself. You radioed that you were putting back to New York because of the weather, so we had the coast searched all the way down. Goodness, how could anybody guess you'd get blown all the way up to this godforsaken neck of the woods!"

She peered into Adam's face, still waiting for a burst of recognition, but he only seemed more baffled. He put a work-hardened hand to his forehead.

"Forgive me, Miss Burke, but..."

"Miss Burke! Oh honestly Peter! Our wedding was to be the society wedding of the year. The ice sculptures were made, the champagne ordered in, and Costains were doing the catering. You have to book them

101

practically years in advance. Mama had the flowers chosen, masses and masses. And then when word came that you had disappeared..."

Her voice trailed off into an appropriate dismay, but whether over loss of her fiance or the difficulty of frustrated caterers, one could not tell. Adam remained bewildered. Aunt Meg and Celia stared the way they would had a leopard – as dangerous as it was beautiful – just walked into their kitchen.

Lydia took a flat gold cigarette case out of her bag and extracted a cigarette. Her hand jumped just a little as thunder crashed overhead but she would not be distracted. She paced in short, clicking steps.

"Peter McEwen, do I actually have to tell you who you are? Taggart's grandson. Taggart Foundries all over the state of New York. Your father sold them, of course, but they still have the name. You used to be the city's number one ladies' man," she smiled, "until you met me!"

"Miss Burke, I'm terribly sorry, but..."

Lydia cut him off with a flick of her cigarette.

"It's all right, Peter, don't worry. I came prepared. I've brought about a ton of pictures to refresh your memory. Oh, and some of your clothes and things you'll need. What is that you're wearing anyway? As soon as this wretched storm is over we can stop at a decent

hotel and get you cleaned up. Then tomorrow –
oh, everyone's agog at the news that you were
found and Mama's dying to start organizing the
wedding again. If we start early in the morning
and drive . . ."

"I can't go!" Adam's voice cut in firmly.
"The farmer here is recovering from an
accident. I'm needed to help out. Tonight
there's still a herd of dairy cows that must be
milked."

Lydia stared at him incredulously.

"Milking? Cows . . . ?"

"Of course. We've just finished a long day
getting the hay in before the rain. And there's
still two more fields to cut."

"You mean . . . they've had you working?
Like a . . . a laborer! Oh Peter, you're not
serious!"

"Perfectly," Adam replied, now regaining
some of his own considerable aplomb. "I
couldn't . . . think of leaving while Mr. Walton
is unable to run things himself."

Lydia seemed to absorb his meaning with
difficulty. When she did, she shot a hard stare
at Celia and Meg, as if they had just committed
some dreadful desecration. And she did not
give up easily. She turned again to Adam.

"But surely . . . surely these people can hire
someone if they need extra help. You don't
imagine you have to stay. Oh Peter, look at

you. All dusty and sunburnt! And your hands! They're just a mess!"

"I've got to stay," the tall man persisted quietly. "I finish what I start."

The finality of his tone killed further protestations. Lydia looked annoyed, and temporarily at a loss until Meg, recovering from shock, bustled to life, filling the kettle and offering this surprise guest a cup of tea and an invitation to dinner. Unable to do otherwise, the city woman decided to make the best of it and hide her former irritation under a fairly gracious smile.

"Well ... thank you, Mrs ... uh, Walton. I am just a bit wrung out from all this excitement. After all, we were *so* sure that Peter was drowned."

The word "drowned" still had power to touch Celia like the lighted end of a cigarette. She winced, dimly aware that she was still in shock. The full impact of Lydia's presence had not yet come to bear.

So while thunder rolled and lightning blazed, and rain fell around them in torrents, the four sat at the old kitchen table sipping tea from thick cups and not touching the homemade cookies Meg had hurriedly set out. Adam swallowed as if he didn't know what he was drinking. Lydia held her mug with the tips of her fingers, as if she feared germs. Celia could not bring herself to taste anything at all. All she was aware of was the inscription from the ring again blazing through her mind. Well, the nightmare had come true. The real Lydia, Adam's promised one, had indeed materialized, come at that very moment to claim the man Celia had foolishly let herself love.

The silence in the room was just reaching the breaking point when, at long last, the fury of the storm began to abate. The thunder rumbled off toward the inland hills, the lightning faded into a distant flicker, and the rain settled into a modest, but steady downfall. Celia jumped up, fumbling for her rubbers and rain cape.

"I'll get the cows," she mumbled. "It's . . . very late."

Adam half rose from his chair, but before he could even offer to go in her place, Celia was out the door and away.

"You stay," she called faintly over her shoulder. "You must have so much to . . . talk over with your . . . your fiancee!"

The word had almost choked her as she slammed the door behind her and rushed out into the gloomy, sodden evening.

Her disbelief was fading now and the real pain setting in.

"Adam," she cried out to the mournful waves as she trudged along the shore. "Oh . . . Adam . . ."

But that wasn't even what he was called any more. It meant nothing. She tried to say his real name. "Peter". It fitted so awkwardly into her mouth. She barely got the sound out past her lips.

A strange new name. For a man now truly a stranger!

Miserably, she plunged along the sand while the waves, lashed into choppy sullen combers, spewed grey foam at her feet. The sky itself, save for a faint flicker of lightning, had settled into a leaden pall of smothering grey from horizon to horizon. Heavy and hopeless. Just the way Celia felt.

The cattle were hunched up wetly under a huge old oak where it was a wonder none of them had been struck by lightning. They were very reluctant to leave their bit of shelter and Celia had to prod them unmercifully before they would start down the muddy lane. On reaching the barnyard, they rushed the open stable door and crowded hotly in. With a pang, Celia realized she had put out no dairy ration.

Yet when she got inside she found each one nosing contentedly in the feed box. The stable lights were on against the gloom and the clatter of utensils came from the milk house. Someone had braved the rain to help.

Ada ... Peter.

Suddenly, Celia quaked at the idea of being

alone with him. Her pail of hot water and disinfectant waited. She picked it up and hurried to ready the cows for the milking machines. She felt as if she could never never bear to look into Ada ... Peter's deep golden eyes again.

She needn't have worried. This transformed man, this Peter McEwen, slipped about the stable like a tall ghost, going about his tasks with rapid, practiced hands while always keeping to the opposite end of the stable from where Celia was.

Oh yes, he was avoiding her just as fiercely as she was avoiding him. The girl bit her lip, trying to pretend the wetness on her cheeks was just left over from the rain.

The pair did not exchange one single word and even Milly the barn cat had to put up a petulant meow before anyone remembered to put out her dinner. When the cows were turned out at the back of the barn where they could take shelter in an open shed, Peter attacked the gutters while Celia scrubbed out the milkers with rapid, shaky strokes. Leaving Peter to switch out the lights, she made her escape and scampered all the way to the house, not caring about the mud splashing to her knees or the rain in her bedraggled, hay festooned hair.

When she got in she found that Meg had opened the doors to the good parlor, although what had induced her to go to this extremity Celia shuddered to imagine.

Lydia had taken it over, installing herself in state on the velveteen settee which was blue green from age but still without any trace of having been sat upon. She had a glass in her hand containing an amber liquid that could be nothing other than a shot of the ceremonial bottle of rye Uncle Bart had kept in the china cabinet for the last seven years, doling out only the tiniest taste at New Year's or his anniversary.

Lydia must have actually asked for some, Celia thought incredulously, unable, despite her year in the city, to shake the local conviction that alcohol on weekdays was the first step to drunkenness, then total dissolution.

Aunt Meg was trotting about getting dinner, her face set in that carefully blank look that said, "you had just better not ask." She was setting an extra place.

"Miss ... Burke," she said, "is going to stay here until ... everything is sorted out. She can have the back bedroom upstairs. It's the quietest, I think."

"Probably just for tonight," put in Lydia from her perch. "Poor Peter. No doubt he'll be much more sensible after he's had a night's sleep."

Meaning, of course, that she expected to

spirit him away in the morning.

As Peter entered through the side door, scraping his feet heavily on the mat, Lydia fished inside her clutch bag until she came up with a set of keys on a gleaming platinum ring.

"Peter, would you be a darling and bring the car up to the door. The trunk is simply crammed with luggage. Just bring in my Moroccan overnight case for now. The calfskin bags are yours. You certainly do look in need of something to wear."

She wrinkled her classically straight nose at Peter's dust-blackened shirt and muddy jeans. His boots, apparently, did not even bear speaking about.

Wordlessly, Peter took the keys and went back out. Lydia's eyes shifted to Celia, resting on the girl with a hooded look that missed no detail.

At once Celia became acutely conscious of her bare feet which she had just pulled out of her barn-scented rubbers, and her streaked and grubby jeans worn ragged by the day's frenzied work pace. Her hair was probably a wet corkscrew frizz and her face smeared with mud. The chaff that had worked its way into all her clothes began to make her skin prickle hotly, and she shrank before the green eyes of this woman. Somehow, in all her life, she had never felt so intimidated.

"Excuse me," she mumbled. "I guess I'm a mess. I better go get cleaned up."

Astonishingly, Lydia broke into an amused little laugh.

"I guess you better, dear. I didn't know one could get so dirty, even in a barn!"

The words were covered by such a well-bred smile that Celia could only open her mouth in astonishment. Then, when she heard Peter setting down luggage behind her, she realized for whose benefit Lydia had been speaking. Peter stood holding the overnight case and looking baffled. Several seconds later, Celia prodded herself into action.

"I'll take that up, Ada ... Peter. Perhaps," she forced herself to turn to Lydia, "you'd like to see where you're to sleep, Miss Burke."

With a shrug, Lydia fell in behind as they mounted the narrow, creaking stair. The back bedroom had once belonged to Celia's grandmother and had hardly been looked into since the old woman's death. Aunt Meg had opened the window and put on fresh sheets but the air had not yet shed its mustiness. The single old-fashioned lamp when switched on, looked pathetically feeble in the creeping gloom.

Lydia looked about with such clear misgivings that Celia was tempted to assure her that there were no fleas in the bed. Then, leaving Lydia at the head of the stairs to find her own way down, the girl bolted to her own room to strip away the sticky, work battered clothes. The shower salved her briefly, sending a cool blessed wave over her shaken body. She managed to comb her curls into a kind of order and splash her drawn face. But nothing, oh nothing whatever, could be done to ease the terror she felt of losing Adam.

When clad in clean slacks and a pale lime sleeveless blouse, she emerged from the staircase with the half enchanted look of a nymph lost from her forest. But she did not know this. She shrank beside the overpowering elegance of Lydia, for Celia had been in the city long enough to recognize the kind of class that only a very great deal of money can buy. She fled to the kitchen as soon as she could.

Unfortunately, she arrived just in time to meet Adam ... Peter emerging from his small bedroom, also washed and changed though only into his extra tan workshirt and the clean pair of jeans Uncle Bart had purchased for him in town. He avoided Celia's eyes and took up a station where the open space gave a view of the parlor and stood there, arms folded, gazing at Lydia as the woman sipped coolly at her drink.

By the time the four of them sat down at the table it was well after dark and the rain continued to drum monotonously over their heads. Lydia, lifting the glass of water beside her for a sip, stopped in astonishment as Aunt Meg began to ask a blessing. The glass remained suspended throughout the soft words. Lydia's mouth quirked in amusement and, as soon as the old woman was finished, she took a dainty drink.

Aunt Meg had prepared a hearty meal, intended as a restorative for Celia and Adam after their frenetic day racing the storm. There was rich broth, a gigantic fresh salad, broccoli, green beans in butter, home-grown beef from their freezer.

But Celia could not think of the food. She was only aware of the chips out of the worn dinnerware, the cream and sugar bowls which did not match, the heavy farmhouse cutlery, the oilcloth table cover with parts of its pattern worn off. She shrivelled inside at what Lydia had to be thinking about all this.

Adam, or Peter, might have been eating cardboard for all the attention he paid to what he was putting into his mouth. Lydia picked languidly at the salad. Celia had all she could do to swallow a couple of mouthfuls for her Aunt Meg's benefit. The old woman presided at the head of the table, ramrod straight, doing her duty as hostess with as few words as possible.

When the rich marble cake was passed

around for dessert, Celia reduced hers to a shambles with her fork without actually eating any of it, though marble cake was her favorite and she knew it had been made as a special treat.

Now all she could think about was the sidelong glances Lydia kept casting at Peter, as if she couldn't wait to get him alone, to draw him into some private, tender reunion. The idea stabbed so cruelly at the slim girl that she stayed only long enough to clear up the supper dishes before she pressed her palm to her forehead.

"I think I'll go to bed now," she got out in a thin voice. "I'm very tired and ... I think I've got a headache coming on."

This was quite true. She murmured goodnight and avoided most of all the look of her Aunt Meg lest it be one of understanding – and pity.

Up in her room the bright pattern of her quilt was swallowed up in the gloom and when the light was switched off an absolute pitchy darkness flooded in, unrelieved even by distant gleams of lightning which had long since disappeared. In an attempt to calm herself, Celia took several deep breaths and stared toward the ceiling.

"I knew this could happen," she said into the darkness. "I knew the minute I saw his ring. If

I've let myself fall into a trap, then I've only myself to blame!"

This was logical, but not in the least bit comforting, no matter how fiercely she told herself she believed it. The dull throbbing ache increased and pounded at her temples. She uttered a low moan. Then the strain of the long frantic day took its toll and she fell into a deep, oblivious slumber.

But even this sleep was not untouched by dreams. Again and again there came the image of the tall golden man high atop the hay, the feel of his strong arms, the first tender brush of his lips across her own.

And when deep in the night, the rain subsided and the clouds let starlight through, it glinted on tears sliding one by one, down onto the pillow below.

CHAPTER FIVE

Morning came, and Celia awoke feeling as if some great weight was crushing her breast. She could not, at first, understand it. Then the memories seeped back – Lydia, Peter, the postponed wedding awaiting them in Boston.

Once again she was forced to relive that

awful plunge when Lydia had first spoken his name. Then, sighing, she thrust herself out of the enfolding shelter of her bed. Her body seemed to ache all over and her hands had blisters where her gloves had worn through. She moved very slowly until a glance at the clock made her yelp and grab for her clothes. It was past milking time already. They'd miss the milk truck. And ... oh, tomorrow she would probably have to do the entire operation by herself alone.

Tiptoeing out, she saw with relief that Lydia's door was still shut tight. Celia felt sure that she couldn't have faced that woman over breakfast.

In the kitchen she found Aunt Meg with a great pot of coffee and fresh scrambled eggs. But the place where Peter always sat was cleared and wiped. Meg saw her looking.

"He went up to get the cows. By the time you get something to eat he'll have the milking just about finished."

Food was about the last thing on Celia's mind, but she sat down dispiritedly and gulped a mug of coffee. Then, as if steeling herself for some terrible ordeal, she stepped out into the rain washed morning to go to the barn.

The closer she got the slower she trudged. Through the stable door she could see the cows lined up in their stalls and hear the rhythmic hum of the milking machines. The barnyard was full of huge puddles. The calves bleated for their breakfasts.

She caught sight of Peter moving among the quiet cows, attending the milkers and laying a familiar hand on each glossy flank as he passed. How much he looked as if he fitted, as if he had been farming all his life instead of just these few short weeks.

Celia watched wistfully, her old automatic impulse making her want to join him, to fall into the easy teamwork they had established since Uncle Bart had injured himself.

But no, the team was forever shattered. The best she could hope was to finish her part of the chores without being noticed.

She entered through the side door and struggled to lift down a great bag of milk replacer. Then she ripped open the top and dished a portion into each of the waiting pails. The calves, taken off the cows almost at birth so that the cow's milk might go to market, thrived on the powdered concoction and, in the fall, would be ready for market themselves.

The calves drank greedily, butting pails and thrusting their heads against the sides so that feeding them required much patience and a firm grip. When the pails were empty they simply bellowed for more.

Celia took the pails to the milkhouse to wash

them and was just about to lift them to their shelves when a swift hand took them from her and put them away. She froze, then forced herself to turn, her breath dying in her throat. Peter was looking down at her, his golden eyes clouded and barely meeting hers.

"Celia ... I..."

"No," she couldn't bear to hear him say it. "No, Peter, you don't have to ... to tell me anything. She found you. It's ... all right!"

"But..."

She began to shake inside. Her cheeks burned. She struggled desperately to keep control.

"Really, P ... Peter. I wish you and ... and Lydia every happiness. I'm just glad that you found out the truth at last."

Quickly, rudely, she turned seeking to escape. Peter stepped in front of her.

"I won't leave," he said quietly. "Not while your Uncle Bart's in bed and there's the rest of the haying to be done."

Oh great. He was allowing them another week or so before he vanished down the road in that glittering Mercedes. If there had been any way, any way at all she could have done the haying by herself she would have begged him to leave that very hour and be done with it. Instead, she only swallowed hard.

"Thank you. That's very ... considerate."

Abruptly she walked away, leaving him to scrub the milking utensils. She drove the cows into the lane before her and soon her shoes were spattered completely as she stumbled through puddles and mud alike.

Halfway up the lane she came to the gnarled pine that had been struck by lightning on the previous night. A great white gash was seared through the bark a good three quarters of the way down the side and the summer green needles seemed already grey from shock. Celia looked sadly up at the blasted trunk.

"I know just how you feel," she murmured. "Oh, I do!"

Since too much water remained from the storm to permit any hay to be cut, all that could be done was to putter about at the odd jobs that had accumulated. When Celia returned from the pasture she found Peter working over the mower in the machine shed. Giving that building a wide berth, she slipped around to see what solace her garden could afford.

The green plot was very much in need of attention. The ever present weeds, encouraged by the rain, were springing up in incredible numbers. Nevertheless, the melon plants had spread their slender vines many feet further, the tomato plants sprawled luxuriously with fruit turning just the palest pink, and the row of sunflowers at the far end had now sprouted higher than her head.

Celia knew she ought to get out the rototiller but right then she couldn't have stood its roar. Instead, she went to the two most delicate rows, the basil and the sage, and with all the tenderness of a mother began to pluck the choking mallow from around their roots. Oh, if only life's other problems could be gotten rid of as easily as a few invading weeds.

The night's storm clouds were now nothing more than a few ragged tatters playing hide and seek with the sun. The oppressive mugginess had all been washed away and the air flowed cool and sweet and touched with the tang of the sea. The ocean had smoothed itself into a shining sheet of aquamarine, flecked with a path of diamonds and trimmed with frothy white lace.

Close to Celia a goldfinch dipped vividly past on black and yellow wings. A monarch butterfly flirted briefly with her shoulder, and the cicadas began to buzz lazily.

Altogether it was a day made for smiling. But to Celia all its brightness was only a mockery. She bent her face away from the resplendent sun and tore yet another handful of ragweed from the moist earth.

About half an hour before lunch she gathered the ingredients for the noon salad and turned reluctantly toward the house. But in the kitchen she found only her Aunt Meg taking a crusty loaf out of the breadbox. Apprehensively, she looked around.

"Isn't..."

"Nope," Aunt Meg's tight mouth showed her opinion of a slugabed. "Not a sign of her yet. Might plan to sleep all day up there for all I know!"

Yet Celia had hardly begun slicing cucumber when a dainty step was heard on the stair. Lydia appeared, stifling a yawn with a hand in front of her already lipsticked mouth.

"My goodness," she declared. "A person could sleep in for a week around here. It's so quiet. Sort of ... creepy, actually. Not a thing going on."

Celia decided she could do just fine without buses honking and traffic bumper to bumper outside the door.

"We're just getting lunch ready," said Aunt Meg, rising to the occasion. "If you'll just sit down..."

"Oh goodness, I *never* eat at this hour. I thought I'd just slip out and have a word with Peter."

Peter was pointed out walking to a storage lean-to, an oily rag flapping from his back pocket, a double roll of baler twine in his arms.

Lydia was dressed, supposedly, for roughing it in the country. That is, in an apricot pant suit which, from the way its long lines accented the lean elegance of her figure, was obviously a designer item. This outfit, along with the high cheekbones, combined to give the impression of a large swift cat, a cheetah ready for the hunt.

An ivory silk blouse, open at the throat, casually revealed a gold chain from which was suspended a large iridescent pearl which was most certainly real.

In deference to the surroundings, she had changed into low heeled Italian pumps with just the tiniest buckle winking on the toe. As she stepped past, Celia caught the kind of perfume whose price tag the working girl dare not even look at. Why then did Celia think the scent reminded her of orchids smothering under glass?

Returning to the salad, Celia made the lettuce suffer unmercifully. But since she was working by the sink, she could not avoid seeing Lydia walk to the edge of the grass and pick her way determinedly through mud and puddles toward the machine shed. Finally, baffled by the sopping ruts where the wagon had driven, she waved her arm impatiently and shouted something. Peter emerged from the machine shed and strode over.

Celia, with a pang, tried to keep her eyes on the salad but could not avoid the two figures in front of her. Though she could hear no words, it was only too easy to guess what was going on.

First Lydia pointed to Peter's greasy knuckles and rough work clothes, managing to convey the depth of her disgust with a flick of her fingers. Peter shrugged, clasping his hands behind his back as if to keep them out of her sight.

The woman launched into an animated speech, gesturing often toward the road and the Mercedes which now sat beaded with rain spots outside the front door. Peter answered slowly, as if he were trying to be reasonable. He looked at the house, not at the kitchen but at the high window where Bart lay nursing his injured back. He pointed to the two sloping fields of uncut hay.

Lydia interrupted, at first smiling, deploying her considerable charms. She even cocked her head and ran a pearly fingernail along Peter's unmoving jaw.

Peter listened gravely. He said something. Her manner cooled and she began to speak more rapidly. Finally, when Peter shook his head, she threw up both arms, turned on her heel, and stalked back toward the house. Peter stood for a long time, staring after her svelte figure. Only when she slammed the side door did he turn, his shoulders oddly slumped and vanished back into the building where he was working.

He wants to go, Celia thought sickly, but gave his word to finish the hay. Now they've had a fight over it.

Lydia arrived back in the kitchen in a considerably worse temper than when she had left it. Going straight to her handbag, she rummaged through it until she snatched out a cigarette and a chic engraved lighter.

She stood motionless for a long moment, inhaling greedily until her lungs could hold out no longer. Then she blew out sharply.

Smoke issuing from the woman's mouth and nostrils did not do a great deal for her looks but it was just what she needed for her nerves. When the first cigarette was done she lit another, sufficiently in command of herself to step back into the kitchen.

"Do you think I could have a cup of coffee," she said in tones that were a virtual command. "I'm simply not alive in the morning until I've had one with my smoke."

Aunt Meg opened her mouth and closed it quickly, deciding not to mention the strong tea that would be ready in a moment. Celia stepped in.

"Just a minute," she said, reaching for the coffee pot. "I'll have some in a jiffy."

Having the farm girl jump so quickly seemed to appease Lydia. She leaned against the door jamb, watching the proceedings with a languid interest but making not the least move to lend a hand. When a mug of strong hot brew was handed to her, she smiled.

"Thanks," she chirped. "Just the medicine. Peter's being difficult today. He never used to be like that, but I guess it's nothing that a little real comfort and good clothes won't cure."

Aunt Meg was biting her lip, a sure sign that she was about to explode. Celia began to dash around, making what distraction she could with the clatter of dishes and the last touches on the salad.

Peter, having previously scrubbed with the strong compound used to remove tractor grease, sat down and ate well, but very silently. But he didn't need to talk. Lydia had changed her mind about lunch, no doubt to sit beside him. She chattered non-stop while she lay one familiar hand on Peter's arm.

A hand, Celia realized, which sported a smaller, more tasteful copy of the ring Peter had worn when he arrived. He made not the smallest move to shake away Lydia's fingers.

There was no doubt about it, even in his work clothes Peter's good looks stood out. It was easy to see that he and Lydia made a handsome couple, that ... they belonged together, that...

Celia felt a hot prickle at the side of her eyes.

She ate her salad swiftly and excused herself as soon as courtesy would allow.

Peter buried himself away that afternoon, working extra hard, replacing the blade on the mower with one that had been newly sharpened, cleaning the temperamental knotter on the baler. For all the world it seemed as if he was hurrying – hurrying to finish the work so that he could slip away with Lydia. Celia wished for the hundredth time that they had never met.

But there was no use wishing. She would have to go through the pain and she knew it. With a heart feeling heavy and wasted, she trudged back to the endless labor of the garden.

That afternoon she scarcely looked up, even when she saw Lydia actually make it all the way to the machine shed to be with Peter. But after about fifteen minutes of standing in the doorway watching him lying on his back, separated from the ground only by a ragged hunk of burlap, tinkering underneath a battered and incomprehensible piece of machinery, the woman gave up and picked her way back toward the house.

She was obviously bored and had no idea what to do with herself in the monotonous quietness of the farm. Celia supposed she would simply go into the house and smoke, but when next she looked around she found herself under the green-eyed scrutiny of Lydia who was barely four yards away. Celia began to hoe all the more furiously, hoping Lydia would grow tired here also and pass on her way.

No such luck.

"What are you working so hard at, dear? You do look a proper country Joan."

"Vegetables. This is our vegetable garden."

"Oh." Lydia took in the rows stretching away from her. "Wouldn't it be simpler just to buy at the store?"

"We like our own," Celia replied somewhat tersely. "Besides, with what we can put away for the winter we can really save some money."

Lydia laughed, but offered no explanation for her amusement. No doubt the thought of people hoarding carrots to save a few dollars was quite droll.

A brittle silence followed. Then Lydia moved a couple of steps closer, lowering her voice.

"Listen, I've been meaning to speak to you – just so you'll understand where you stand. Naturally I didn't miss that little scene you and Peter were playing out when I drove up. Quite touching, even from a distance."

Celia felt her face turn to fire. The hoe shook in her hand.

"I . . ."

"Oh you don't have to explain." The

sweetness in Lydia's voice dripped like acid. "I can see how a little morsel like you could appeal – momentarily – to Peter. Before we became engaged he used to have girls with ten times your style for breakfast. With this amnesia thing, it's natural that he reverted a little." A manicured hand rested ever so lightly on Celia's shoulder. "Just don't think about it. You'll soon forget."

Celia threw off the long fingers as if they were scorpions.

"What Ad ... Peter and I had together you can never guess, Miss Burke! And I'll thank you not to speak this way to me again!"

Lydia raised her eyebrows and stepped back.

"Well, touchy touchy. I was only trying to help you, dear."

That kind of help Celia did not need. Her knuckles were white on the hoe handle as Lydia strolled off across the lawn. No matter how great the lump in her throat she was determined not to let that woman see her cry.

She managed to save the tears for late in the night when she was free to cry into her pillow all she wanted. For the afternoon, she wrought such havoc among the weeds that the garden would certainly not have dared to sprout another one until the haying was finished. She left early to get the cows and spent the interval kicking at the sand as she scuffed along the shore, swearing that she would get Peter's golden fascination out of her mind if it was the last thing she ever did.

The hike to the pasture and back got her blood circulating and proved enough of a distraction so that she felt able to bring herself into the stable with Peter to take up her milking chores. She found him checking the thermometer on the cooling tank. He did not look up when she entered.

It was quite amazing how they got the same work done yet managed to do it separately, avoiding each other meticulously, never crossing each other's path. They were like two strangers who had never met.

After the cows were turned out, Peter scrubbed the utensils and left them solemnly out for Celia to put away while he took up the shovel for the gutters. While reaching to hang up a milk pail Celia was alerted by a warning prickle on the back of her neck. Turning, she found Lydia in the doorway.

The farm girl was taken with a powerful impulse to bolt, but she gritted her teeth, refusing to be rattled. Taking care not to let any part of the milkhouse touch her satiny sleeves, Lydia stepped inside.

"Cleaning up, I see," she murmured as she swept past into the main stable where Peter was at work. She reached the connecting door before her face took on a ghastly look and she froze in her tracks.

"Peter," she screeched. "Oh Peter, what ARE you doing?"

Peter looked up from his aromatic task, his face going tight.

"Well," he sounded defensive, "it has to be done."

And with a few swift strokes, he finished it, washed the shovel and stood it in its place against the wall. All the while, Lydia did not relax the horrified astonishment on her face.

Celia felt her own cheeks heat. She could not help remembering the first time Peter had done that job, his delighted, goodnatured laughter ringing out.

"There seems to be something ... screamingly funny about me pitching in on a job like this!" he had said.

Well, now she certainly knew why. And Peter knew. No more merry laughter. He had finished up in grim silence as if, knowing who he was, he felt ashamed. Embarrassed to be seen by his high-toned fiancee. No doubt he wished he were a thousand miles away from such menial work.

And soon, very soon, he would be!

After Peter had rinsed off his boots with extra care, he and Lydia made their way off toward the house and supper. Celia, not wanting to be a tagalong, hung back, arriving only in time to see Lydia pushing Peter gently but firmly toward his own bedroom door.

"Darling," she said, "it's time you put on some of your own clothes, don't you think? At least for the evening. I've laid out a few things on the bed."

With only the faintest hesitation, Peter went in and closed the door behind him. Celia turned away, not liking to think of Lydia unpacking his personal things, handling them intimately, running her fingers across cloth his skin would touch as if ... as if she were Peter's wife already.

The girl's stomach tightened. She wondered if ...

She wondered about things that were definitely none of her business. Heading for the kitchen, she went to help Aunt Meg with the meal.

Peter seemed to be gone a very long time. But when he did emerge Celia felt a long breath slide out of her throat.

"Oh," cried Aunt Meg in spite of herself. "Oh my!"

The old Adam in rough jeans and tangled hair, had truly stepped through a looking glass and turned into this sleekly groomed, heart-stoppingly handsome Peter. The unruly hair had been combed into a rich sweep which, though it had grown out a little, did not belie the lines of its expensive cut. His grey slacks showed their quality by their soft, unerring fit and the two creases were sharp as the blades of knives. His shirt was dark green, and lay against his skin with the whisper of silk, bringing out the deep bronze glow of his tan.

He was, in fact, the man-about-town reborn – the polished manners, the well-groomed elegance, the easy set of his shoulders. He needed but a cocktail glass to complete the picture.

He simply stood there, looking about, the old wry smile banished under a look of casual indifference which seemed, oddly enough, to more clearly define the aristocratic planes of his face.

"There, darling," Lydia said, obviously pleased, "now you look like your old self. Really ... those awful jeans you were wearing!"

Gliding forward, she took both his hands in hers. Then she looked down and gave a little cry.

"Oh Peter, the ring! The ring I gave you! Don't tell me you've lost that too!"

Celia's mouth went dry and a terrible constriction took hold of her chest. As Peter shook his head she had to look away.

"No ... no," he murmured. "I haven't lost

131

it. I ... took it off some time ago."

"Well for heaven's sake, do go find it. You can't leave a piece that valuable just lying around in some corner, you know!"

Mildly, he went into the bedroom and returned with the great ring flashing its red and white fire in the palm of his hand. Perhaps he expected Lydia to put it in her purse for safekeeping. But Lydia had no such notion. Taking Peter's hand, she slipped the heavy gold circle over the knuckle and onto his third finger, turning it up so that it winked and glittered in the soft evening light.

"I will admit," said Lydia, "that it is a bit gaudy, but when the Coles went bankrupt those stones were such a bargain. Remember the way people stared at our engagement party!"

Peter frowned and looked at the floor. Lydia paused, then let out a little laugh.

"You poor dear," she crooned, stroking his shoulder. "You're still so mixed up, aren't you? Well, just wait until you see all the pictures I brought. They'll straighten you out for sure."

The prospect of showing them seemed to put her in a good humor. She bantered lightly with Peter all through supper. Later, while Celia washed the dishes and cleaned up, Lydia brought a large dark leather case from the Mercedes and opened it up on the parlor table.

A veritable wave of newspaper clippings, photographs, and momentos spilled out of it. She placed Peter on one side of her and just as Celia had hung up the dish towel and was about to escape to her room, she touched the sleeve of the country girl.

"Oh Celia, do come and sit down too. I'm sure you'll find all this just fascinating. It's so different from what you're used to."

Remembering the scene in the garden, Celia wanted to hiss, but Lydia had now got her rather firmly by the wrist and drew her down into a chair.

Celia knew why, of course. It was just another way to harp on the distance between the girl's modest farm life and Peter's world. However, once down, Celia did not seem to have the will power to get up again. She stared at the jumble in the case. Some compulsion held her, making her desperate to see, even second hand, the glittering circle in which Peter properly belonged.

"I raided positively everything," Lydia laughed. "Even your family albums, Peter. See, here you are as a little boy of maybe six or seven years old. I did draw the line at baby pictures on the bearskin rug!"

She extracted a formal colored photograph of a solemn blond child staring fearlessly into the camera. With a dignity beyond his age, he carried off a navy blue suit complete with little waistcoat and an impeccably knotted grey tie.

The two flanking figures, Lydia pointed out, were his parents. The mother could more properly be described as handsome, with a broad brow, fine eyes and a firmly modeled chin. It was a strong face – a determined face, one might have said – had not the whole effect been spoiled by a thin mouth hesitating in a most uncertain smile.

This hesitancy was instantly compensated for by the man, Peter's father, who was possessed of such rivetting good looks that even Celia could not suppress a tiny gasp. This man beamed broadly out of the picture, his arm thrown casually across his wife's shoulders, his rosy bloom and telltale puffiness hinting at a fondness for a tipple and a roaring good time.

The fourth presence was a portrait on the wall behind the family group, a painting of an older man with the same fair hair and broad brow as Peter and his mother, yet utterly devoid of the easy, well-dressed refinement. He folded a pair of huge rough hands defiantly over his vest. He glowered out on the world with a fierce scowl that seemed to burn into the very nerves of the spectator. His mouth was a line of steel that seemed to say, "Just dare!"

Peter gazed at these figures intently, knitting his straight brows but saying nothing, not even when Lydia explained that the grim portrait was his grandfather.

"That's Hamish Taggart. The one that came from Scotland on a cattle boat or something and built up all the foundries. Here's one taken a few years ago, after he had his stroke."

A second photograph showed the same man, only now he was shrunken, white-haired and appallingly thin. He was wrapped in a rug and parked in a wheelchair on some blurry patch of lawn. The same fierce gaze remained, but the self-possession had been replaced by an elemental bitterness. His was the face of an aging eagle, deprived of his wing feathers, ending his days on the end of a chain.

Lydia sighed.

"Funny that your parents should be dead and this old boy is still hanging on in that nursing home. Can't do a thing but sit and stare. That time you took me to meet him I could feel the creeps running all the way down my spine."

Oblivious to Lydia's comments, Peter stared at the photo as if it had reached out and gripped him with claws. For a brief moment his eyes burned with a fierceness that matched that of the old man and the muscles of his jaw stood out in knots.

This look was swiftly replaced by one of confusion. He shoved the portrait away from him, out of sight under a pile of others. But his jaw did not relax until Lydia had slid a number of other items in front of him.

"Oh, here you are in the Commodore Cup yacht race," Lydia laughed. "The way you knocked yourself out to get your hands on that cup!"

This was a newspaper clipping, carefully sealed into a plastic sleeve. On one side it showed a swift white yacht tilting into the wind, every inch of canvas crowded onto the mast. Beside it, in a close-up, Peter grinned mightily, a yachting cap cocked over one eye, his hands lifting an enormous silver trophy.

"Wealthy playboy waltzes off with Commodore Cup," clucked the headline. "Practically a steal!"

"Too bad about the Sea Wings," Lydia put in. "But really you could hardly turn around in her. You promised to take me shopping for something we could cruise in. I've always wanted to see St. Tropez from my own cozy yacht."

Celia breathed out slowly as it began to dawn on her just what kind of people Lydia and Peter actually were − not merely well-heeled, not merely affluent, but rich, rich, rich! They could shop for a luxury yacht the way Celia shopped for a bathing suit.

Rummaging through the pile, Lydia picked

up a bundle of clippings then tossed them impatiently aside. Peter retrieved them and fanned through them curiously.

"Oh," shrugged Lydia, "that's just a lot of dull stuff from ages ago. They're all about when your parents sold the foundries. My secretary must have thrown them in by mistake."

Secretary, thought Celia as the headlines sped by. "Taggart Industries on Block." "Daughter, Son-in-Law Lack Interest." "Cash Liquidation Produces Fabulous Sum!"

As Peter slowed down she began to pick out bits and pieces of smaller type: "... industrial empire built up from a single machine shop...", "... paralyzing stroke forced founder to relinquish control...", "... heirs cash in their chips, opt for the good life...", "Grandson Peter, teenage hellion..."

Lydia slid the packet from Peter's hand and flipped it into the case.

"Really, foundries are fine, but I don't blame your parents for taking the money. What's the good of being rich if you haven't time for fun!"

She found another clipping and her face lit up with a smile. It was a large shot of Peter in a velvet tuxedo, with Lydia draped over his arm. She was waving with the condescension of royalty while the neckline of her gown took a glittering plunge almost to her navel.

"Peter McEwen, Lydia Burke announce engagement. Wedding promises to set Boston on its ear," said the caption.

After this came a whole page of pictures from the engagement party. Glittering people milled from wall to wall, champagne glasses were hoisted aloft, and everywhere, everywhere Lydia was managing to smile into the camera, each time looking more pleased with herself.

And Peter! Oh, this was not the steady, good humored man who had worked in the hay, but rather some stranger laughing tipsily, tossing off glasses of bubbly.

This was too much. Celia could not bear to go on looking at the man who had so entangled her heart. Her chair scraped as she rose and Lydia turned instantly, her hand darting out.

"Oh don't run off now, dear. There's plenty more."

The glint in the long green eyes hinted that she was more than aware of the pain these pictures caused the young girl. Celia prised herself away.

"I'm sure there is, Miss Burke, but I ... I have a headache. I think I'll just go and lie down!"

A flicker of triumph at having driven the girl from the field passed over Lydia's face. For a moment Celia could not bring herself to leave, thus conceding defeat, even though Lydia turned back to Peter.

"Are you remembering now, darling? Are things coming back?"

Peter let out a long sigh. Then, rising from his chair, he took a few abrupt steps, his hands going to his forehead.

"I don't know. It's just ... everything's so foggy and ... oh bother it anyway!"

Celia stared in spite of herself at seeing the confident man she knew reduced to this uncertain turmoil. Lydia frowned, either in puzzlement or annoyance, and picked up another handful of pictures.

"Even with so much to remind you, Peter! Well, sit down. We'll go through some more and ..."

"No. I don't want to look at any more. Not ... tonight!"

He turned to Celia so much in the old way that for a moment the girl's heart jumped, expecting one of his familiar smiles.

Instead, his eyes slid past her face, his scowl darkened, and he shouldered by, all but knocking her against the door as he strode outside into the pale lemon afterglow of the sunset, the great ring winking on his knuckle as he went. Lydia very deliberately locked all the papers into the case and walked out after him.

By now Celia really did have a headache. She looked into the small old sitting room only to have Aunt Meg peer up at her over her spectacles in undisguised sympathy. That was too much. Quickly she retreated up the stairs to her room.

She felt so drained that she got into bed immediately, but sleep refused to come. Peter's rude exit had hurt her more than she cared to think. But why should he notice her now that he had his fine society bride!

Each time she tried to close her eyes she had a stabbing vision of Peter and Lydia standing out under the maple, drawing into each other's eager arms. Peter's old life was reaching out to him, leaving nothing for Celia save the memory of a golden god atop the hay and one heavenly pain-torn kiss under an apricot moon.

Through her open window came the distant wash of the waves. At first they seemed to mock her. Then, to Celia's dazed mind, they became like tears upon the shore.

By morning she knew that the only possible way to survive the remainder of Peter's stay was to keep as far out of his path as possible. During the haying she would do what had to be done. After he was gone she would be left alone to heal – as best she could – the horrible hole in her heart.

It would be worse than after the loss of Gavin. Ah, Gavin! With a pang, she realized that she had not thought about him for weeks.

Once she had cared for him deeply. But now he seemed more like a charming boy beguiling her time until she found the man she was fated for, the one true love of her life.

Peter was eating hash browns and bacon in the kitchen, silent as a carving, hardly taking his eyes from his plate. Lydia, of course, was nowhere to be seen. When he stood up he only flicked a glance at the bright sun rising over a countryside so innocent of all traces of the downpour.

"Going to be clear," he muttered. "Good chance to cut another field."

In the stable he worked faster than ever but with a robot-like efficiency, as if his mind – and his heart – were somewhere else altogether. It was easy for Celia to avoid him. She could only sigh with relief when at last she was alone, taking the cows up the lane to their salt-tanged seaside pasture.

On the way back she dawdled, scuffing her toes, and poking at hummocks with a stick until she saw the tractor and mower pull out and make their way to the gate of the hayfield. The two remaining meadows were quite small. It should all be over in a few more days.

With the mower racketing through the hay above her, Celia knelt among the cucumber vines, seeking out the tiny gherkins. She would spend the afternoon helping Aunt Meg to put up jars and jars of dill pickles Uncle Bart loved so much in the winter.

This day Lydia managed to sleep clear through lunch, emerging to sip a cup of coffee only in time to see Peter off to the fields again with his tractor. For a while she stood on the doorstep, trying to decide whether or not to follow him up the lane. But there is nothing very gripping about seeing a tractor and mower going around and around inside a tiny field. And inside there was a most annoying bustle of pots and jars, not to mention the overpowering smell of hot brine, which made Lydia cough in disgust.

She went back to her room and, in a very few minutes, emerged dressed in a white skirt, a mint blouse frilled at the neck, and a long strapped purse. With barely a nod to the two women working in the kitchen, she got into the Mercedes and sped off down the gravel road toward Harrisburg.

Peter finished the field just after four o'clock that afternoon and was scrubbing at the grease on his hands when the silver car purred back. Lydia jumped out in a much better mood than when she had left.

"Oh Peter," she called, nimbly avoiding a smudge of oil, "I found this perfectly delightful little restaurant. A French fellow runs it. He's a real chef. We simply must go there for dinner tonight. I'm withering up of boredom here and . . ."

"The milking," Peter cut in quietly. "I can't go anywhere until . . ."

"Oh bother the milking! Surely these people can do *something* by themselves!"

Celia, who had been on her way to the house with another basket of gherkins, stopped, open-mouthed. She wanted to explode, but to do so would be to reveal that she had overheard Lydia. The country girl backed behind a lilac bush as Peter said something that couldn't be made out.

"Oh all right," Lydia snapped. "Hurry up and do whatever it is you have to do. But I told Gaspard we'd be there at six. Don't blame me if the dinner is spoiled!"

Gaspard's! The special little place where Peter – Adam – had taken Celia that first time they had gone to town. Oh trust Lydia to discover the one place Celia couldn't bear to see them go!

In the kitchen, Lydia announced that neither she nor Peter would be around for dinner.

"After all those pickles," she grimaced at the lingering smell, "you probably won't want to eat anything anyway."

Aunt Meg almost dropped the bottle of dills she was carrying, but managed to control her tongue. Celia slipped off the blue apron that was tied about her slender middle and left by the side door. If those two wanted to get started early she had better round up the cows.

Taking shelter in the mournful solitude of the shore, she padded along towards the pasture. The cows looked up from their grazing, startled and indignant at being rushed. Once in the barn the waiting dairy ration pacified them.

Peter worked so fast that Celia had to conclude that he was in a hurry to be done with the chores and away with Lydia. Celia strained to keep up with him. He scraped out the gutters, cleaned the milkers and loped off to the house. When Celia brought herself to follow him, she opened the side door and all but gave herself away by a stifled croak of surprise.

Lydia was obviously dressed for a night on the town. She paced – or rather stalked – about the parlor waiting for Peter to get ready. As she walked, she swished a severe yet breathtakingly elegant cocktail dress. It was in a burgundy so deep that it seemed to glow with a luster all its own, proving all the more marvelous a foil for Lydia's satiny, pampered skin. The top was sleeveless, with only a gather at the shoulder to prepare for the dramatic neckline plunge down to ... well, down to the chunk of silver embedded with green emeralds that flashed with every breath she took.

Her hair, brushed into its polished cap, swept up into an exquisitely cut curve just above the lobes of her ears which sported, in miniature, two perfect replicas of the glittering brooch on her bosom.

Celia's entrance made Lydia pause and glance at the girl with a small half smile about her lips as if she was quite aware of the effect she was creating. Then she lifted her head, haughty as some princess bestowing for a moment her presence upon that humble dwelling. People, she seemed to be saying, ought to be grateful just for the privilege of looking at her!

"Do you think I'll be warm enough," she asked, twisting the knife ever so daintily. "I could get my shawl – Seville lace – I had it made up in Spain for the honeymoon."

Celia's throat constricted as if it had been clutched by a fist. The height of her mortification was that Lydia knew she could not answer. The woman did a small half turn. Touching the brooch at her breast to make sure it was noticed, she set her classic profile against the light of the window.

"It'll do Peter good to get out tonight," she drawled. "We'll get the kind of food he's used to, and take it easy. The way he looks, he could certainly do with a change."

Her eyes raked pointedly over Celia's faded

jeans, garden-stained shoes and blue shirt from the discount sale.

"He *has* had a change," Celia said, somewhat acidly. "Perhaps it's done him more good than you imagine!"

She turned away, ready to help with the modest dinner – and all but ran head on into Peter as he emerged from the small side bedroom.

Celia forgot to move. He was even more breathtaking than Lydia. Gone were his jeans. Instead, he wore slacks and a jacket of some deep amber color that closely matched his eyes and highlighted the deep bronze of his skin.

His shirt was cream silk, touched at the neck with one dash of flamboyance – an ascot that was made from a deep wine material that picked up the shade of Lydia's dress. Lydia was nothing if not a superb stage manager.

The bantering, hay-festooned Adam that Celia had known was a million miles from this lithe creature in fine clothes, and softly curling hair. Now he looked simply magnificent, beyond all doubt the real Peter McEwen, man-about-town.

When the silver Mercedes had sped off, as incongruous as a space ship on the narrow gravel road, Celia turned from the window, her slim shoulders slumping.

"Don't make much for me," she told her

146

aunt. "I'll just have a little soup and take a tray up to Uncle Bart."

Escaping to the bathroom, she splashed her face then searched her wardrobe for a fresh blouse. This was a depressing exercise, for her few simple clothes hung there looking cheap and dowdy. Even the soft beige wool A-line she had bought for Gavin's birthday party and the little gay pink sundress she had worn to town with Adam seemed horribly inadequate. Oh, she thought, slamming the door in despair, Lydia wouldn't even use those things to clean the windshield of her car!

She went to the kitchen for a bowl of beef broth and a chunk of crusty brown homemade bread. Then she prepared her uncle's tray.

"He's restless as a flea on a griddle up there," Meg said. "So don't you let him try to get up. Not now, with his back coming along so famously."

Uncle Bart was indeed fed up with his confinement. He wasn't much of a reader, so after the local papers had been exhausted and a magazine or two had been leafed through, he was at the end of his patience. His face lit up when Celia came in.

"Here's your dinner," she said cheerfully. "Soup and sliced ham. We're eating light tonight."

The old man harumphed.

"Sure. Great way for a fellow to starve to death."

"Oh come on. You've been waited on hand and foot. A royal holiday is what you're having."

"Sure looks like it from this meal," he remarked, a gleam in his eyes. "What's the matter? Her ladyship isn't eating with the common folk tonight?"

Celia's grin faltered.

"Uh ... no. She and ... the two of them have gone out to a restaurant."

"Oh." Uncle Bart shifted himself up and took the tray on his knee. "I thought I saw that showboat she drives going down the lane."

Celia said nothing, and he sampled the soup.

"I met her," he continued in a somber tone. "Meg brought her in and she looked at me as if I were a warty toad. All her nice manners couldn't cover what she thought."

"Yes, she is a little ... strange. She's not used to ... this kind of life, I guess."

"Huh, strange isn't the word. It's a wonder she hasn't choked on our food by now."

Celia looked down at her knuckles.

"Well, there's not much for her to do around here and ..."

"I guess not! She's itching to get away, I can see that. Adam ... Peter's real good to stay on until I can get around. And anyway," the sight of his niece's lowered eyes made him try to be hearty, "I'll be out hopping around like a spring tadpole any day now."

Celia's grin was tremulous and oddly lopsided.

"You bet, Uncle Bart. Sure you will!"

She knew only too well that the old farmer was trying to cheer her up. It was his way of saying he was sorry about the way things had turned out. His shrewd eyes had picked up more about her and Adam than ever she had imagined.

After the tray was set aside, Celia spent most of the evening playing checkers with her uncle and trying not to think of a certain little restaurant table overlooking a rose garden. Gaspard would be hovering there, giving Lydia the same attention he had once lavished on her. The candlelight would throw Peter's profile into glorious chiselled relief. Lydia would lean across, laying one of those long white hands on his wrist while at her breast the emeralds flickered . . .

"Hey, wake up, girl. I just jumped three of your men in a row and got a king. You're going to be wiped out!"

Halfheartedly, Celia attempted to save her rearguard. It was useless. Bart quickly won, then folded up the board.

"I'm getting tired of this anyway," he lied.

"Why don't you just run along to bed."

Expecting Peter and Lydia to be out until all hours, everyone retired early. Celia lay in her bed and listened to the moan of the sea, her mind assaulted with all the things she imagined to be going on inside the Mercedes. Oh, she wouldn't be surprised if the loving couple didn't come back until dawn.

But just as she was closing her eyes in final weariness, the slam of car doors jolted her and the front steps creaked shortly afterwards. Peering at her little illuminated clock, she saw with astonishment that it wasn't even midnight!

CHAPTER SIX

The next day, under steadily increasing heat, Peter raked the hay. He was almost totally silent now and only paused to remark that since the weather was so dry they could begin baling almost immediately.

Before the hay could be brought in, however, there was the problem of moving the elevator around to the opposite side of the barn to fill the second half of the mow. Uncle Bart issued elaborate instructions and even went so far as to ease himself into a chair by the window to point out what had to be done. With only Peter and Celia, the job would be tricky.

Aunt Meg took up a post on the veranda and Lydia watched the proceedings with growing horror.

This task, if there were to be no accidents, was one that required Peter and Celia to work together in absolute co-operation. All thoughts other than those concerning the job at hand were banished.

First the long metal elevator had to be detached at its upper end and lowered foot by foot onto the flat body of the hay wagon. Peter climbed into the crammed loft, braced his feet and took hold of the stout rope he had attached to the end. Carefully he let the metal structure slide down the side of the barn.

"That's it," he cried as Celia, poised on the tractor, moved the wagon under the elevator as it sank so that it came to rest across the middle, perfectly balanced.

"That's just great!"

The vigor in his voice recalled a little of his former zest. When he climbed down, he steadied the elevator with his arms while Celia guided the whole unwieldy outfit, at a crawl, around the barn. Once at the other side she backed up, watching only Peter's hand signals, to exactly the right spot below the second loft door.

Again Peter climbed high in the barn, having to balance this time on a long ladder since there was as yet no hay to stand upon, and ran the rope through the pulley.

"All right," he called down. "Just hold it steady and back up as I raise it. I'm going to pull the end up now with the rope."

The elevator, though deceptively thin, was a heavy piece of equipment. No one had ever raised it by hand. The rope had always been attached to a second tractor.

"But . . ."

"Don't worry. I can do it. Just keep that wagon straight!"

Amazingly, he grasped the rope and pulled, his chest muscles standing out in great bands under his work shirt. Slowly, evenly, hand over hand, he actually lifted the elevator to the eaves of the barn and secured it to the small chain hanging ready.

"There!" He was actually grinning. "Nothing to it! By tomorrow we'll have bales in by the wagonload!"

Unconscious of anything save their moment of shared triumph, Celia laughed back, coppery tendrils of her hair blowing along her flushed cheek.

A second later, as if they had come abruptly to themselves, Peter's face went dark and he vanished into the shadows of the mow. Celia's mouth drooped. With a sigh, she took the wagon around to park it in its accustomed place.

She returned just in time to see Lydia pounce on Peter as he emerged from the barn doors.

"Good God, Peter, what are you trying to do – ruin yourself? You don't have to slave like that for anybody! If they're so helpless why don't you just hire a man for them. Then we could leave this..."

"Lydia, I promised! I don't want to hear..."

They both fell silent when they caught sight of Celia, her cheeks hot with confusion. Peter walked stiffly off. Lydia shot a venomous glance at her before striding away toward the house. Minutes later the engine of the Mercedes leaped to life.

Celia bit back her tears and sought her old refuge, the garden. She picked a few blackberries, thinking they might have them for dessert, then abandoned the project because the birds had all but stripped the bushes clean. The few in her hand she tasted. Then, remembering them crushed in Adam's strong white teeth that first day, she threw the remainder on the ground for the birds to eat. Since there seemed nothing else to do, she walked along the shore to bring back the cows for milking.

Oh, she thought, if only she could hold her tongue until that woman was out of the house!

Despite the fact that she had scuffed her toes in the sand the whole way, she arrived early. She leaned over the gate to watch the glossy holsteins settled in the grass, chewing their cuds and dreaming grassy dreams behind their drowsing eyelids.

Well, Celia thought bitterly, this certainly can't compare with the excitement of Boston or New York. Just the same old routine day after day – get up, do the milking, take the cows to the pasture, bring the cows back from the pasture, do the milking, wash out the milkers, feed the cat. And in the evening, if you're not too tired, you get to sit on the veranda and listen to the grass grow while the sun goes redly down in the sea.

How unutterably dull ... and ... how lovely!

Yes, lovely, Celia declared to the cows. It had taken her a year away from home to realize how content she could be living within her own garden borders and breathing the wonderful salt air of the pine studded Nova Scotian coast.

Oh sure! And the ghost of her drowned Gavin, plus the memory of a tall golden man swept forever away by the glittering whirl of his New York life would make great company!

"Come on, girls!" She swung open the gate,

"Let's get going."

The cows heaved themselves up with reluctant grunts and headed patiently off, still chewing their cuds. Celia followed, her stomach tight over the prospect of meeting Peter in the stable.

Though the milking was not really more painful than at other times, Peter had become incredibly silent. He carried an atmosphere around with him as dense and chill as an arctic fog. Once, when he accidentally bumped into Celia, his apology seemed but a grunt as he shouldered away. As he finished up with the gutters his face seemed frozen into what looked like permanent distaste.

A wave of humiliation rose inside Celia as she watched. It's degrading to him, she thought, now that he knows that he's Peter McEwen. The millionaire. He can hardly wait for Uncle Bart to get well so he can get himself out of here.

Despite the place set for her, Lydia did not come back from Harrisburg for dinner. She was obviously eating out. But when she did return, about an hour and a half after dinner had finished, she had cooled down enough to put on a good face. She even smiled at Celia and Aunt Meg.

She greeted Peter warmly, taking his arm and inviting him, quite pointedly, for a walk along the seashore. It was clear she was out to mend her fences with him and Peter went along without question. From the window Celia caught glimpses of them far down the sand. Lydia, clinging to Peter's arm, was talking with great and charming animation. Peter walked gravely, his head bent, as if each word his fiancee dropped had for him some deep but obscure importance. Then, when they went out of sight around a headland, Celia supposed he'd take Lydia in his arms and ...

Oh, hadn't she sworn to keep such thoughts from her mind? But how could she forget the sight of Lydia – magnificent in her burgundy dress, emeralds at her bosom, a diamond on her thin, manicured fingers. It only took a look at her own hands, calloused from baler twine, nails worn to the quick, skin brown from days and days in the sun, to reduce her to despair.

He's ... ashamed of me, she thought all in a rush. Ashamed of ... of having made advances at a time when he wasn't ... quite right in his mind. Now that he sees Lydia, now that he knows the world he belongs in, he probably can't bear the sight of me! I'm nothing to him now but an unfortunate embarrassment!

This idea was the final misery. She wished she could creep away and hide until both Peter and Lydia were long gone from the humble farm.

There was, however, no such escape. The next morning the hay had to be baled. Silently, Celia climbed up into her seat and started the baler, glad that the ear-assaulting din drowned out all possibility of conversation. For though they continued as before, it was as if some kind of invisible wall had been established between them.

The heat had been increasing steadily. It was not the rain-bearing mugginess preceding a storm, but a high blazing summer heat which made the land bake into a gigantic hay-scented furnace. Since the field was small, they finished just before lunch and brought the machinery back to the barn. When they went to the house to splash water in their faces and gulp down quantities of icy lemonade, they could not help but look around for Lydia. Aunt Meg jerked her head toward the shore.

They looked out of the window. Sure enough, there was Lydia laid out on an enormous beach towel. Her hair was wrapped in a turban, her bikini was bright yellow, and her eyes were protected against the sun by some mask-like contraption.

"Got up half an hour ago," said Meg. "Said she might as well try out the beach." The old woman sounded glad about anything that would keep Lydia out from underfoot.

Since it took time to convert the tractor for

the hay loader, Celia and Adam only managed to get one load onto the wagon that afternoon before it was time to stop and think about the milking. They had just run the last bale up into the barn and were trudging back to the kitchen for another desperately needed drink when they met Lydia strolling up from the sea, her towel draped over her arm, and her turban swirling up like icing on top of a cupcake.

When she saw Peter her walk became infused with a conscious feline grace. Her body glistened with suntan oil and the bikini made her look like a swimwear advertisement from *Vogue*. She smiled lazily.

"It's not the Riviera, darling," she drawled, "but one must find *something* to do around here while you're puttering with those ridiculous machines."

Four thousand bales of hay cut and stored! Puttering! Lydia had probably lifted nothing heavier than her make-up case in her entire life.

The milking that night was more silent and uncomfortable than ever. At dinner, Lydia picked at her food as usual and Celia expected her to hustle Peter away somewhere as soon as she could.

Instead, Lydia got out the case of clippings.

"All right, Peter," she said brightly. "Let's have another look. You too, Celia. I don't suppose you'll ever get the chance to see the kind of parties we have!"

Celia immediately declared that she had to go and play checkers with her uncle. She did, in fact, go upstairs and get two games in before Bart grew drowsy and threatened to doze off over the board. He could sit in a chair now and stated his intention of trying the stairs the next day.

Leaving him to his nap, Celia tiptoed downstairs again, hoping that Lydia would have tired of memory lane. But this was not the case. Before the girl could slip past them into the kitchen, Lydia adroitly got her by the waist and drew her to the table, chirping that Celia "simply must" take a peep at all the lovely pictures.

This was, of course, Lydia's not-so-subtle way of baiting the girl, but Celia could find no way to refuse without laying her hurt open for all to see. Stiffly, drawn by a painful desire to peep into Peter's world, she sat down.

Since Lydia had picked the pictures out, most of them were of herself in various stunning outfits at various stunning events. Peter, handsome in flawlessly cut suits or dramatic in evening clothes, was usually at her side, the carefree man of leisure.

Only in a couple of photos, where he had been caught unaware by the camera, did he show a different face. In one he just frowned moodily, a drink forgotten at his elbow. In a second, he leaned against an elaborately carved mantelpiece, surveying a crowd of dancers with a queer, sardonic twist to his mouth.

But these two were surely exceptions. The rest of the time he moved through this glittering whirl with consummate, laughing ease.

Celia's heart shrank but she could not bring herself to move away. Lydia shuffled through the heap with increasing impatience, finally handing an unopened wad of clippings to the girl by her side.

"Be a dear and hold these, will you? I just know there are some of the derby meet at the bottom."

Celia held the bundle as if it burned her, for it seemed to consist entirely of engagement notices. The headlines leaped up at her: "Handsome Couple to Exchange Vows" "Engagement Party One of the Grandest" "Boston Aristocrat Nets New York Money".

That last one caught her. The paper was cheap and grainy, as if from some scandal sheet. The printed paragraph pulled no punches:

". . . proof that the ravages of inflation are driving Boston blue bloods out of their closed circle. Miss Lydia Burke, whose

160

weakness for high fashion and fast living are well known, has sidestepped her family curse of debt and bad investment by adroitly reeling in the fabulously wealthy Peter McEwen. McEwen's uneducated grandfather, whom the Burkes would not have spoken to, built up an industrial empire with his bare hands. Now, when all around, old family money is crumbling and present day scions have to actually work for their..."

"Oh, what on earth is that!" Lydia had noticed what Celia was reading and snatched the papers out of her hand. "Honestly, that secretary of mine clips things from the awfullest rags!"

Deftly, with a sidelong glance at Peter, she peeled off the offending sheet and crumpled it to nothing in the palm of her hand.

Then she quickly lit upon a large color photo featuring herself, in a dazzling turquoise evening gown, along with Peter and several other people in front of set of palatial doors.

"Oh look," she cried. "That was at the opening of Benny's play. Such a wit! And there's the Graysons!" Her finger pointed to a plumpish rake leering slyly at the slinky looking woman on his arm. The woman was smiling at the camera and letting the tip of some horribly expensive piece of fur trail on the pavement. "You remember Jack and Lucy Grayson, surely!"

Lydia looked hard at Peter, with narrowed eyes, willing an answer. He looked a long time at the couple, then nodded his head.

"Yes, I do. He's the one who danced on the bar at the party after. And Lucy ... she has this dreadful little Cairn terrier that's addicted to champagne..."

"Right, Peter! You're perfectly right!" Lydia was all but crowing with triumph. "You do remember. Lord, what a relief. I was really starting to worry, you know!"

Unable to move, Celia felt her heart plummeting like a hunk of limestone. Her last forlorn hope, unknown even to herself until this moment, had been that Peter would remember nothing and that this had all been some ghastly mistake. But now Peter truly had his mind back. The farm – and herself – would be no more than an awkward wrinkle in his glamorous life. At the worst it would be an embarrassment not worth mentioning. At best, it would be a funny story to make the Graysons giggle over their gin and tonic.

Her hands fell to her sides. Unnoticed by Lydia, who was too delighted to turn her attention from Peter, Celia glided up the stairs to the refuge of her seaward room.

The days that followed only confirmed her painful knowledge. The old Adam who had kissed her under the moon was now completely obliterated by this stiff, unsmiling Peter. He very rarely spoke. He allowed himself to be led off without protest any time Lydia felt like a stroll on the beach or an evening in town. He communicated with Celia only when necessary and then only in monosyllables.

Of course, they had to work together. But they did it now as if each moment was some private agony. When they came near each other they clattered pails or dropped something to forestall conversation.

While Peter worked in jeans and an open shirt, Celia could only see him as he was in the pictures – tall elegance in a tuxedo, raising a champagne glass in his hand. As the scent of new milk and clover drifted through the sweltering stable, she glanced at him sideways. I bet he's counting the minutes, she thought. I just bet he is!

She bit her lip with the unfairness of it. After all, when those fancy people put cream into their bone china coffee cups, where did they think it came from anyway!

Her one effort to take over the most undignified of the tasks, the cleaning of the gutters, had met with an abrupt end when Peter had taken the shovel roughly from her hands.

"I've been doing until now," he muttered. "I can certainly finish it!"

Feeling as if she had been slapped, Celia retreated from his sight.

In spite of the merciless heat, the two of them worked relentlessly to bring in the hay from the second to last field. Whatever agonies they may have been suffering from inside, none of their outward expertise, their old well-oiled team effort, had diminished. In perfect unison they lifted, stacked, unloaded, and stored away. Celia always set the bales on the wagon exactly where Peter needed them. At the elevator she paced herself instinctively so that bales would neither overwhelm the man in the barn nor leave him staring impatiently at the empty conveyor.

Lydia, despite her forays to the beach and her sessions with iced tea and fashion magazines under the shade of the maple, watched the work closely and could not miss the sophisticated co-operation that had developed between her Peter and this solemn-eyed farm girl. A few times she crossed the barnyard to watch the unloading process, and once went so far as to walk up the shaded lane to see the two of them clearing the stubble.

Each time her green eyes narrowed and her mouth pursed. But she never lasted longer than five or ten minutes before the blistering heat and the repetition of the work snapped her patience. Taking care that her Siamese batik wrap didn't get smudged, she would shift from one foot to the other for a moment or two, then make off toward some shady refuge and the tall cool drinks Meg had to keep in supply.

Celia would cast a parting glance after the haughty figure picking its way over dandelions and trampled plantain.

You needn't look at me like that, Celia thought mournfully. There's no danger here. Nothing is the way it looks. Neither of us can wait to get away.

She then stole a glimpse at Peter who was working high atop the rising load. Even with the sun on his hair and his powerful muscles rolling as he swung the bales, he seemed but a ghost of the old Adam who had laughed up there and labored with delight, untroubled by thoughts of work below his dignity. Perhaps it was only an illusion of tear-misted eyes, but it seemed to the girl that Peter's joyous golden light was damped. He was shrouded, closed – waiting perhaps until he could get home to where his brilliance really belonged.

By early afternoon the field was cleared and the mower hitched up to fell the small stand of hay that remained. Once that bit was raked and baled and put away in the barn . . .

165

Refusing to think about it, Celia worked furiously among the potatoes when she wasn't required in the field. The weather, out of either kindness or perversity, was co-operating perfectly, providing torrid cloudless days which, though they stiffled the breath and sent the cattle deep into the woods for shelter, made ideal drying conditions for the hay.

Uncle Bart had now left his bed completely and, when he wasn't enthroned on the ancient porch rocker, was walking gingerly about, seeing how everything was getting along. Dr. Morgan had been out in the morning and had nodded thoughtfully.

"You're a tough old bird, Bart," he chuckled. "Getting better a lot faster than I thought you would, even though I couldn't keep you in your bed. Anyway, just don't you go lifting anything until I tell you. Shouldn't be too long now."

Grudgingly, Bart agreed, though anyone could see he was itching to be back on the job. More than anything, he hated sitting around like a lump on a log. Especially, he confided to Meg, with that snooty Boston gal prowling about like a cat on tacks.

Lydia was indeed restless. She had not expected the enforced stay at the farmhouse and chafed visibly, though she would not take herself and her shining car off to a hotel,

166

leaving Peter alone with Celia.

She got slightly sunburned at the beach which she insisted, in a temper, was full of stones and wretchedly narrow. She had exhausted the rather scant attractions of Harrisburg and now spent her time, when not pacing restlessly, immobile under the maple surrounded by creams, lotions and glossy magazines. She seemed to have a dozen bikinis and made sure Peter got a good look at her in every one of them. In the evening she fanned herself with her handkerchief.

"Really," she complained, "I just don't see how people *exist* without air conditioners!"

When the last of the hay was baled and ready to be drawn in, Lydia began to revive. She visited Celia and Peter as they finished up one afternoon with only a couple of loads left out on the stubble.

Even she could tell that the haying would be done the following afternoon and she cast a calculating eye at the field. As Peter headed to the house for a drink, Lydia fell in beside him, stepping carefully so that her Italian leather sandals would not become caked with dust.

Celia, as usual, dragged far behind – but not far enough to miss what Lydia was saying. Lydia's voice, with its pear shaped Boston tones, could probably have cut through glass at forty paces.

"Well, darling," she smiled, laying her hand on Peter's arm in the gesture that had become her own "Private Property" sign, "I see you'll have all that beastly hay finished tomorrow. I suppose it'll take the whole evening to get the smell of cows off you, so if we start out early the following morning we shouldn't be that long hitting New York. I'll phone the Graysons and Mama and..."

Peter broke in on her, making a short gesture and muttering words Celia could not pick up. With an inflamed face she tried falling even farther back, but still she could not escape Lydia's voice.

"What are you talking about! Of course we're leaving! That old man and his niece can get along just fine and they ought to be bloody grateful that you've done as much as you have, if you ask me!"

Then Peter was saying something in a low voice and his shoulders had become very hard. Celia didn't wait to hear any more. Trembling with mortification and suppressed rage, she fell back toward the garden and spent a good many minutes pacing the cabbage rows before she could bring herself to enter the house behind the other two.

When she did, she found Peter out of sight washing up and Lydia's petulance replaced by a very smooth smile.

"Well, we'll be off day after tomorrow for New York. And I guess," she gave a tiny flutter of a laugh, "you'll all be glad to have us finally out from under your feet!"

Aunt Meg and Uncle Bart remained tactfully silent. Celia, her breast chokingly tight, made a movement with her shoulders which she desperately hoped was a shrug. She refused to let Lydia see her suffering. And no matter what the woman had been like, she would not be rude to a guest so late in the stay.

And yet . . . and yet . . . one more day, a few more loads of hay, and Peter – Adam – would be gone out of her life forever!

Oh, she cried out inside herself, oh my darling!

Dinner that night had to be the most dreary meal Celia had ever forced herself to sit through. The few remarks that Meg and Bart tried to make fell as flat as chunks of lead. Peter ate with his eyes on his plate. Lydia, despite her former confident brightness, now seemed possessed by nervous restlessness. She sipped half a cup of tea, picked at her vegetables, and excused herself shortly to smoke in the parlor that had been kept permanently open for her convenience. As soon as Peter scraped back his chair, she was upon him.

"Do let's run into town for a drink, darling. I'm just . . . jumpy as a cat sitting around here

169

with nothing to do."

She did not appear to have seen the stack of dishes on the counter. Celia began washing them up with a furious splash and clatter. By the time she was drying them, Peter emerged from his bedroom, heartrendingly handsome in a chocolate shirt and tan jacket. Lydia, shimmering in a dress of some smokey sapphire material that clung to her somewhat angular curves, bore him off triumphantly by the arm.

A minute later the silver Mercedes purred past the window and down the lane.

For a split second Celia had the terrible impression that he was gone for good, on down the road to New York and the rich, easy life where he belonged.

Blessedly, she fell asleep almost the instant her head nestled into the pillow and could not tell what hour the two of them came in. Again she overslept and found Peter almost finished with the milking. Tightly silent, he opened the gate to let her take the cows into the lane. When she returned she found him with the haywagon, apparently impatient to be done with the job so he could take his leave.

Unable to speak, unable even to look at him, she drove up to the field to begin.

From then on every passing moment, every bale shunted onto the wagon and packed into place, was a stab in Celia's heart. Peter worked hard and quickly but without zest. His face was fixed into a stern, inward expression, his thoughts in some distant glittering place where Celia could never hope to follow.

All morning they worked, filling the loft while the elevator clattered and bales fell with a heavy thump on top of their fellows below. At lunch Peter ate very little but gulped long draughts of the spring water kept beside his place. Lydia, who had been up all of two hours, nursed a cigarette and looked curiously smug.

Well, it wasn't hard to imagine why. She was to have her fiance all to herself at last and the big wedding was back on schedule. Celia bit her lip and excused herself so as not to fall victim to wet eyes at the dinner table.

One more night, she thought, one more night!

Oh well. She drew a deep breath and tried to steady herself. She had known the odds. Right from the beginning she had known the odds. All that was left to her now was to be as brave a loser as she could.

There was only a load and a bit left in the little field and swiftly, oh too swiftly, it was lifted from the stubble and transferred to the barn.

The mower, the baler and the rake, Celia knew, all sat inside the machine shed, greased and oiled and set in order for the long storage until the following year – or more likely, until the auction when Bart and Meg were finally forced to sell.

All that remained of the haying now was the task of taking down the elevator. Celia and Peter repeated the operation of a few days before, lowering the long conveyor until it was flat on the wagon. This too was backed into the machine shed where, with the help of a pulley, Peter hoisted it up to the rafters and suspended it from hooks so that it would be safe from rust and rain.

When the rope was taken off, he turned slowly to Celia who was waiting on the tractor seat.

"Well," his voice was low and just a little thick, "I guess ... that's that!"

Celia trembled, unable to move – hoping, expecting a word, a sign, some little gesture of private farewell. But he only hopped heavily to the ground and disappeared into the shadowy depths of the barn.

In dismay, Celia watched him go. Then she realized it wasn't yet time. There were the cows to milk and all the evening's preparations for the departure in the morning. He would be with them yet a few more hours.

The impulse came as she unhooked the wagon and put the tractor in its garage. If the milking was the last task they would share together, at least she would not do it in her ragged old work jeans and faded shirt stuck full of hay. She would wash her face and comb her hair and put on that lovely pale green blouse she loved so much. She didn't care if she was going to wear it in the stable.

Darting up the back stairs, she washed with the sandalwood soap she had received for her birthday. She donned the blouse, slipped into her new jeans and combed her hair, all the while managing not to look directly at the drawn little oval face in the mirror.

She got back outside the same way she had come in and was about to start across the lawn when a movement caught her eye. It was Lydia, who was packing the Mercedes with luggage. The trunk was full and the back seat was taking its share. She wore the same expensive suit and high-heeled shoes that she had arrived in.

In fact – she was dressed for traveling!

Not that evening, not tomorrow, but right now! She did not even intend to wait for the milking. She meant to grab Peter the minute he appeared and make off with him directly.

Celia felt tears stinging at her eyes and didn't know what to do. If she stepped out it would be practically into Lydia's path and one, just one of those casual cutting remarks...

Oh ... and there was Peter, walking swiftly

toward Lydia and the car. Celia shrank back behind the corner of the old grey house.

Peter was grease to the elbows and caked with hay dust, but this did not deter Lydia. She slid directly in front of him.

"I've packed all our things, Peter and we're ready to go. If you'll have a bit of a wash, there's a change laid out for you on that bed you were sleeping in. Those dreadful rags you're wearing can go straight into the garbage."

"Packed?" Peter sounded incredulous. "You packed?"

"Why yes! I'm sure you're dying to get out of this, well ... hovel as much as I am. God, you can't guess how bored I've been, stuck with only that pokerfaced old crone in the house. We can stop at a hotel tonight and have a real soak in a tub. I can't stand being nice one minute longer to a bunch of hicks and that backwoods girl who wouldn't know a dress if she saw one!"

Hicks! Old crone! This after Lydia had been taken into their home and treated to their simple best!

Lydia's laugh, now unpleasantly shrill, snaked out on the afternoon air. For one horrible second Celia thought she was going to dash out there and attack that woman.

But Peter was there! Was he smiling too?

Was he chuckling smugly at Lydia's colorful descriptions?

Oh it would be too much! Too, too much!

Unable to think of anything now save the blind pain and humiliation in her heart, Celia turned and fled through weeds and tangled grass and whipping shrubs until she skidded down the bank onto the shore.

She ran until she was exhausted, stumbling through the pale hot sand, panting until she dropped for support upon a flat-topped rock. Gavin's rock. Not caring how she bruised her knees, she climbed to the top and sat staring miserably out at the sun spangled sea.

The smiling, deceptive, treacherous sea, flashing its diamonds at her, spinning its elegant whorls of snowy foam lace – this sea had done it again. It had brought her heartbreak. It had washed up at her feet a shining golden man who had taken her love and crushed it with a shrug. What was he but fool's gold, a dazzling trick to beguile, then wound her foolish hungry heart!

Helplessly, Celia drew up her knees and sat with her head down on her elbows, her forehead resting against her wrists. High overhead a gull cried out.

The ruthless sun blazed down onto her unprotected neck, laying its hot brand upon her skin, but Celia didn't care. All she could think about, all she wished, was that never, never had she ever heard of Peter McEwen.

And yet...

And yet there had been all those good times; the laughter in the hayfield, the wild, exhilarating race against the storm, the feel of his powerful arms...

No! She mustn't think about those things. She must think about nothing at all. She must sit perfectly still and make her mind into an untouchable blank. It was her only defense against the pain washing in on her from every side.

So she sat, fighting a silent but desperate battle not to sink deeper and deeper into the dark pit of misery that yawned before her. Her lips pressed tightly together. She grew too absorbed in this grim inner world to notice the soft, all but soundless steps approaching in the sand. A tall shadow fell across her body. A hand touched her shoulder – a hand which had the effect of an electric shock.

"Celia." The rich note trembled through her. "Celia?"

For one petrified second she supposed it but another trick of the sea. Then her head jerked up. Adam!... Peter!

Yes, of course. Her mind backpedalled furiously. Peter ... come to say his last goodbye.

Struggling desperately to draw a breath, she hoped her cheeks weren't spotted with giveaway tear stains. She tried a feeble smile.

"So ... Peter ... your memory came back after all."

His face was very intent, and oddly bright.

"Indeed it did. I remembered plenty more than I wanted to. And ... I found out why I wanted to forget."

Celia blinked.

"Why ... that cut on your head! The storm ..."

"More than the storm. More like Lydia."

"Lydia! But ... weren't you sailing to your wedding?"

He ground his heel sharply into the sand.

"Yeah, sure. But I felt like I was sailing to my doom. So I guess when the storm upset me I chose to block out everything and ... start over."

Celia's eyes flew open wide.

"You what!"

Peter frowned and began to pace a little, his hands clasped behind his back.

"Well, you know my life story. Mom and dad got control of the foundries and sold them off. After all, why worry about a business when you could just trade it in for cash. Dad could talk mother into just about anything. He saw life as one big long spree and brought me up to think the same. Why not! We could afford it!"

Peter paused, looking out at the sun-flecked sea.

"Oh, I can't say I didn't enjoy it. I did. The only person who could upset me was my grandfather, glaring at me from that wheelchair as if I were some kind of pup. I never knew why until I washed up on this farm, Celia."

"But ... why wouldn't the old man be delighted with his only grandson?"

Peter laughed shortly.

"Not a grandson he regarded as about as useful as a flea on a lady's ear. Grandad, you see, worked himself up from nothing. He kept working right up until his stroke. Then he got stuck with a son-in-law who did little and a grandson who did less. He was disgusted. And so was I, I guess, after my parents cracked up their private plane. Only I didn't know what was wrong with me. With all the luxury and money I had, everyone said I was the luckiest man around. On top of that, I was pursued by one of the Boston Burkes. What a connection!"

The tall man began to pace more quickly now, his face full of memories.

"I just went along, thinking I was crazy to be dissatisfied. But as the wedding got closer I had this tight feeling, as if I were being squeezed but I didn't know by whom. One of the reasons I went on alone in that yacht in spite of the weather was to try and think things out once and for all before Lydia got her chain around my neck."

"And then," he turned to Celia with one of his golden grins, "I woke up in your spare bedroom, my mind a blank. I was happy here, Celia, really happy – because I learned to work. For the first time I found out what grandfather had that I didn't – respect for himself. He had been useful and I was but a parasite. No wonder he glared at me."

Celia struggled to absorb all this. Like most people in the world, she had little idea of the troubles of the super rich.

"But ... if you've got money, you don't really need to work. You can..."

Peter turned to her fiercely.

"Oh yes I do! Long and hard, just the way we were doing before Lydia drove up. It took me a long time to figure this out, and I'm afraid I've been ... terribly rude sometimes. But just now, when Lydia started sneering at your family and expected me to jump into that car with her like some trained poodle, I knew I never could. Never again!"

Celia sat bolt upright, her legs sliding over the side of the rock. Suddenly her heart was pounding inside of her.

"Aren't you ... isn't Lydia?"

Peter smiled very slowly; and pointed. Far

above them, where the little dirt road wound into the uplands, the silver Mercedes was racing toward the highway, lashing an angry tail of dust. In wonderment, Celia turned to the smiling bronzed man whose hair glinted in the sunlight and whose eyes swept her into their golden incandescence.

"No," he breathed. "I'm not going with her. I'm not fool enough to leave the one girl that I love."

Celia felt the breath die out of her as, for the first time, she noticed that the hand that had pointed was again bare of Lydia's glittering ring.

"You mean ..." her voice was faint as the whispering sea breeze, "you want ... me?"

He came to her, his sinewy hands taking her shoulders.

"Celia ... that night in the storm, when all the currents were against me ... it was the light from your window that gave me hope, gave me the courage to keep swimming. It was a beacon for my life, for my heart. I want to stay, to farm, to build a stone house up there on the headland for ourselves and all our children. My money could do much here that needs to be done."

It was then that Celia felt the stars, the pinwheels exploding inside her. Her lips parted. Her eyes were luminous with that inner light only love can give.

"Oh ... oh, my darling..."

He gathered her to him in one tremulous melting kiss. His work-hardened arms clasped her against his chest. The sunlight fell over them like a blessing.

Celia lost herself, her singing heart telling her only one thing. This was no trick of the sea, no fool's gold.

It was the real thing!